THE PLIGHT OF A SCOTTISH LASS
Clans of Mull, Book 1

THE PLIGHT OF A Scottish Lass

CLANS OF MULL • 1

KEIRA MONTCLAIR

FOREWORD

TO MY LOYAL readers,
I've changed a few things in this novel since it's a new series. Less Scottish dialogue, less steam, and a brief twitch into a new genre. I hope you'll stay with me!

And I welcome any new readers. If you like this series, I have fifty books that revolve around the lives of three generations of Clan Ramsay and Clan Grant.

Whatever brought you here, please stay, and let me know your thoughts! I'm always listening.

I chose the Isle of Mull as the setting because there are records of medieval castles there.

The primary castle, Duart Castle on the promontory of the Isle of Mull, is listed as the seat of Clan MacLean in the 1350s. Before that, research shows conflicting stories. Some places claim the castle was built by the MacLeans, others claim it was built by the MacDougalls.

MacDougall fell out of favor with King Robert, and since that fit my fictional version of the story I wished to write, that's what I'm going with for this series. King Robert the Bruce awarded the castle to Clan Ramsay (entirely fictional), who dubbed it the home of Clan Grantham.

Welcome to my new stand-alone series—Clans of Mull.

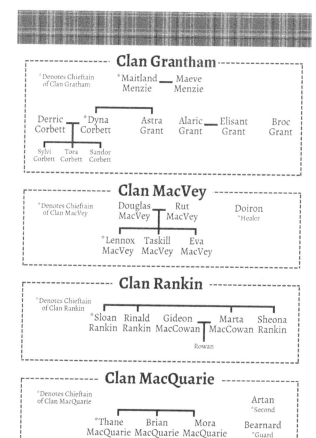

Clan Grantham

*Denotes Chieftain of Clan Gratham

*Maitland Menzie — Maeve Menzie

Derric Corbett — *Dyna Corbett

Astra Grant

Alaric Grant — Elisant Grant

Broc Grant

Sylvi Corbett   Tora Corbett   Sandor Corbett

Clan MacVey

*Denotes Chieftain of Clan MacVey

Douglas MacVey — Rut MacVey

Doiron *Healer

*Lennox MacVey   Taskill MacVey   Eva MacVey

Clan Rankin

*Denotes Chieftain of Clan Rankin

*Sloan Rankin   Rinald Rankin   Gideon MacCowan — Marta MacCowan   Sheona Rankin

Rowan

Clan MacQuarie

*Denotes Chieftain of Clan MacQuarie

Artan *Second

*Thane MacQuarie   Brian MacQuarie   Mora MacQuarie

Bearnard *Guard

PROLOGUE

"NEWCOMERS ON THE Isle of Mull? I fear they'll not be here for long." The man's fist flexed on his sword's hilt.

"Why not?"

"Because I'll kill them if they get in my way. I will control all the inhabitants on the isle. They will do as I say or regret it." His long hair feathered back in the evening's summer breeze that wafted through the trees as if warning them of an incoming threat. But he wasn't worried. Despite being younger than the other man, he requested his guidance based on his renowned wisdom. His age implied unparalleled experience.

No one would stop him.

"Who are they?"

The older man explained, "It is said that King Robert the Bruce gifted the castle to Clan Ramsay. Since the MacDougalls deserted the castle, it is now a gift to his favored clans. They are fierce fighters, strong archers, and have assisted Scotland many times. Even their women fight."

The man snorted, his derision of the fairer gender something he never tried to hide. "I do not fear them, especially their women. How many are there?" He strode over to a large boulder and climbed on it for a better view of the isle that would belong to him someday. He lacked sufficient men for now, but his coin would soon rectify that. This incident of new tenants to the castle was a minor complication, nothing that worried him. "How many?"

"I'm not sure. I've heard their weaponry is formidable, with more en route. It surely will take them a while to build a force strong enough to protect the castle." The older man walked over to a row of bushes and relieved himself, tossing his weapon into the tall grasses next to him.

"I will not worry about them. They are too small a force to concern me. What else do you have?"

"Unfortunately, that is where you are wrong. You should concern yourself. They will be a formidable enemy because the curtain wall is nearly a horse's length thick. The sea walls the MacDougalls built are some of the thickest I've ever seen."

"But as long as their numbers are low, we will persist."

"There are several groups on the isle. How do you expect to overtake them all when they are so far apart? They sit on four coastlines, one inland near the mountains. I can't comprehend your belief in overtaking such a large number. You may defeat each one by day, but then what will happen when you move to the next one?

Their proximity makes it impossible to control all of them unless you have ten score more men at the ready."

"If we kill them all, there will be no one left. Then we will have their riches. Horses, sheep, cattle, gold coins, seed, furs, and unlimited weaponry. You'll see. I am not ready yet, but when I am, I expect your support."

"You have it. Just send me word when you are prepared to attack."

"Do you have any other information of value?" The old man was wasting his time. He could have learned most of this if he'd visited the castle on his own.

"I have. One woman is a healer. Both women are archers, and one is said to be the granddaughter of Gwyneth Ramsay. Her husband is the grandson of Alexander Grant. The other woman is the daughter of the Grant laird. If you kill either, expect the wrath of Clan Ramsay and Clan Grant to fall upon you quickly."

"I do not fear any clans, and why should I care about someone named Gwyneth Ramsay? That name means nothing to me."

His acquaintance chuckled. "She was once the finest archer in all the land. Once pinned a man to a tree by his bollocks. They say this one is as fierce. Protect your jewels when she is around."

The man grinned. "I look forward to meeting her. If she's a healer, I may have to keep her. We do not have one, and they do have their value." He mounted his horse and turned the beast around. "Did they bring horses?"

"I heard they have two warhorses and one mare."

"Warhorses. I can surely use a couple of fine stallions. This is good news. Until our next meeting." The man sent his mount into a fast gallop.

The second man climbed on his beast and left. This was the second fool he'd learned of who thought they could take over the Isle of Mull easily. One was the brother of the chieftain of Clan MacDougall, but this one? He wasn't quite sure who was backing him. And without a large force behind him, he'd never be successful.

The MacDougall, he'd just been shamed and was without any coin to feed his fetishes. And a wee bit daft. One shouldn't forget that large piece of his personality. Daft meant desperate. But this one? He wasn't sure he understood what was driving him. But he would uncover the truth of it.

Once they were both gone, a lad stepped out from behind a tree and spit in both directions. "I must meet the newcomers, my friend."

He glanced over his shoulder at his companion, then grinned.

CHAPTER ONE

Tamsin

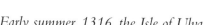

*Early summer, 1316, the Isle of Ulva,
Scotland*

"YOU WILL GIVE me a son this time, or
I will kill you." His arm swung in a fast
arc, slapping her cheek hard, her head bouncing
off the stone wall from the force of the blow. She
took a deep breath, heaving a wee bit, something
that helped her keep her cries inside.

Tamsin would not react, no scream or tears. If
she did, she knew from experience that a second
blow would follow.

"My lord, how would I do that?" She was but
eight and ten. How did one make a child in
your belly a girl or a boy? There must be a way
that she did not know. But first, she needed to
make herself with child again. Was there a way to
guarantee the brute's seed would take again? She
was so naïve about the ways of women and men
that the topic embarrassed her.

Every eve she prayed it would happen again
soon so he would go to another's bed. She hadn't

had her courses in a while, so she was hopeful, but her belly hadn't grown yet. The reprieve she'd had once since she'd had an enormous belly from carrying their daughter was something she hadn't expected.

She enjoyed the privacy immensely. She hated the act. The brutality of it, the way her husband hurt her, tested her strength every time. She'd rather he had three other women to bed if he would leave her be.

The next blow caught her in her belly and came from his fist, so powerful it knocked her off her feet and she landed on the table behind her.

The servants gasped behind him.

Unable to see clearly, Tamsin huddled into a ball, her hands cradling her belly. Something was wrong. Terribly wrong.

"Extilda," he called out. "Take Alana and send her to my mother's house."

"Nay," Tamsin shouted, attempting to sit, but unable to because of the pain from the blow that still gripped her insides. That she could tolerate—beatings, neglect, starvation, even imprisonment. Her only wish was to not be kept away from their daughter. "Please, my lord. I will keep her quiet." She adored wee Alana.

He grabbed her by the hair and lifted her off the table. "You will not see her again until you bear me a son." Then he shoved her back.

Only this time, she missed the corner of the table and slid off the edge onto the floor, landing on her side. A trickle of blood burst from her womb, a warmth washing between her legs. She cradled her belly, a sudden fear engulfing her. She hadn't even known she was carrying.

A serving woman yelled, "Get the midwife! She will be delivering."

Raghnall bent over and spit on her. "A son. Remember that it must be a boy." The sound of his footsteps on the stone floor told her he was leaving. She peeked around him when the searing pain struck, the kind that told her a bairn was on its way. One she wasn't aware had been inside her.

The servants had called her plump, ungainly, and foolish. Her husband had called her unlovable. Why hadn't she realized she'd been carrying again? If only her mother had lived long enough to explain such things to her instead of having to learn the intimate truths from serving girls.

Blushing, a thought came to her she wished to deny. She hadn't wanted another bairn except to keep her husband at bay. Suppose she had a lad resembling Raghnall. What if her husband raised a boy who resembled him in every way?

"Alana. I want Alana," she whimpered when the woman helped her to her feet.

"Come. You will surely lose this one. You are not far enough along. The midwife is on her way. Do not make matters worse for yourself." The woman pinched her arm as if to enforce her instructions.

Tamsin pinched her back.

CHAPTER TWO

Eli and Alaric

Near the Isle of Mull, Summer, 1316

ELISANT RAMSAY GRANT leaned over the bow of the ship, the wind whipping the random strands of burnished gold freed from her plait, but she ignored the mess the climate was making of her hair. The beauty of their journey was more than she could have expected, and she vowed not to miss any of it.

"Alaric, have you ever seen anything as lovely as this?" She reached up and brushed the blond strands from his face, the journey wreaking havoc with his long hair. Since he was the most handsome man in the Highlands, she loved staring at him, especially the way his muscles moved when he practiced his sword skills. His goal was to have the same reputation his uncle Connor had as a swordsman—the best in the land.

Alaric wrapped his arm around her shoulders, tugging her close before he dropped a chaste kiss on her forehead. "Aye, I have. The beauty is quite close to me."

Eli elbowed him with a grin and replied, "I mean it. Have you seen the sea before?"

"I've had a lovely view of the water near Roddy and Rose's castle, and it is quite stunning, but not like this. And if you look north, you can see Loch Linnhe. This is so unique, so…mesmerizing. That's it. It makes me want to never tear my gaze away."

She ran her fingers down the side of his chiseled jaw. "I have never seen the sea before, husband dearest. This is a first for me. It's stunning. The water, the waves, the sparkles when the sun pops out enough to shine its rays upon the glorious sea. I don't know which I love the most." Then she leaned in to whisper in his ear, "Imagine making love on this rocking ship. Would it not be an experience?"

Eli loved the physical part of their marriage as much as Alaric did. She didn't know why people were uncomfortable discussing that part of a couple's life because she loved it.

Alaric squeezed her hand, nibbled her earlobe, then whispered, "Aye, I would, but we cannot. Stop thinking on it or you will embarrass me."

He gave her a pointed look that made her glance at his trews, then she tossed her head back and giggled.

The boat was a birlinn, the sail doing most of the work at present because of the wind, but the oarsmen were at the ready.

Maitland Menzie joined them at the bow as their vessel sluiced through the water, their destination the Isle of Mull. Maitland, at seven and thirty, was the eldest of the group, his brown hair and full beard making him look more mature than Alaric. He was ten years older than Alaric, but the gleam in his eye made him a favorite of many. "There it is," he declared, pointing to the distant glimpse of land ahead. "Duart Castle. Our home for the next few years."

"You'll miss Maeve, Maitland, but she'll be here soon enough."

"I already miss my sweet wife. I'll stay for a sennight, see what supplies you need, then return to Cameron land. Whatever we need, I'll bring along on the next trip, and I hope that the day will come soon when Maeve and our son join me. But I'll do what is best for all. Maeve insists on it. She said she didn't think I would enjoy sitting and staring at her gigantic belly while she's in her last months."

"I cannot wait to meet him," Dyna called out from behind them. "Come here so you can listen to what the captain says about our destination." She tugged on her nearly white hair, held back with a tie high on her head. At thirty, she and her husband Derric were the middle-aged couple.

Alaric took Eli's hand and tugged her from the edge, though it was difficult to pull herself away from the gorgeous view of the sea, the island in front of them, and the distant castle that was to be their new home.

The four of them had fought together at the Battle of Skaithmuir, a decisive battle between the Scots and the English. Ever since King Alexander III had passed on in 1286, the two countries had battled over territories and castles, especially around the Borderlands. Robert the Bruce had led the charge to win the Scot's independence, but the two still battled over lands near the border, especially Berwick Castle. Sir James Douglas led the Scots' charge in King Robert's absence. Maitland and Dyna had been given the responsibility of protecting the land of the Scots while Robert assisted his brother in Ireland. The Scots had sent the English running after the battle, and their king had been pleased.

In return for their loyalty and diligence, King Robert awarded them Duart Castle on the Isle of Mull, a fine castle that was presently deserted. He'd warned them of the unrest on the isle. Multiple incidents of thievery had disrupted the usually peaceful group of clans, though the guilty parties had yet to be caught.

In order to achieve peace on Mull, he requested the Ramsays assume control of the castle, familiarize themselves with the residents of the land, and take the necessary actions to halt the attacks and incessant reiving that had been brought to his attention.

The collection of allies—Grants, Ramsays, Menzies, Camerons, Drummonds, and Mathesons—had gathered and decided who to send to the island, thus choosing the group of six.

Alaric Grant, newly wed to Elisant Ramsay.

Derric and Dyna Grant Corbett.

Maitland Menzie and his recent bride, Maeve Grant, who was about to deliver their first bairn. Maeve would join them in a couple of months.

It was an exciting endeavor, something that had Eli hopping out of bed every morn, waiting for the day they were to meet their destination.

The captain of the boat was someone who ferried people from Oban to Craignure, a place down the shore from Duart Castle, and thus was more than familiar with Mull.

"Captain, what do you know of the residents of the isle? What are the most populated areas? What clans?" Dyna asked.

The captain grinned. "Och, there are many. Clan MacVey and Clan Rankin are at the northern end—MacVey in the center near Glen Aros, Rankin in the northernmost point near Tobermory. I've heard of one clan of crude inhabitants to the west, Clan MacQuarie. But they are not overly hostile to my knowledge. They live on the western coastline, close to the sea and the other isles and keep to themselves mostly."

"Have you ferried them anywhere?"

"The MacQuaries? Hell nay, not with the ships they have. They look like the longboats of the Norse. Probably repaired some left from the Battle of Largs years ago."

"Do you ferry to the south?" Alaric asked.

"Nay, just two spots on the northeastern coast. I go to Craignure and to Ardmore Point near Bloody Bay. That spot is close to Clan Rankin."

"And no one has inhabited the empty castle?"

"Nay, not that I've seen. The castle was built by the MacDougalls, but they are not supporters of King Robert, instead supporting the Comyns.

They argued, met King Robert in Argyll, and never returned, instead choosing to stay where they had more protection. The castle has been empty for less than a year. There are MacClanes in the southern part of the isle, and word is they wish to take over Duart Castle, but it has not happened yet. So, you become the new residents of the castle by the gift of our king, and the MacDougalls can do naught about it. I wish you much good fortune. It has quite a view, so they say, sitting on the promontory as it is. High enough to see eye to eye with the eagles and falcons, of which we have many."

Eli's gaze drifted back to the castle that grew larger and larger as they skimmed across the sea. "Do they swim in the water there?" she asked, since she'd always loved swimming in the loch near Ramsay Castle.

The captain laughed. "Of course they do, but not right off the point. You might want a more protected spot down the beach. And south of Duart, there are some incredible beaches. You should look for them. The water is mighty rough on the point. You'll see soon enough. I'll not try to go ashore there but instead take you to the port of Craignure. There's a small village where you can meet some of the local people, pick up supplies, or grab an ale at the inn."

"Perfect," she whispered, resting her head on her husband's shoulder. How her life had changed in such a short time.

The ship docked at Craignure on the Sound of Mull. The captain pointed up ahead. "There is a nice path from here that goes through town, and if you head south, it will take you straight to the castle. Directly to the keep. You'll find it clear, but it will take you a wee bit to carry your supplies. I'll get the horses from below deck. Once I get them out, we'll find a place to leave the crates, and you can carry some later. There aren't many who would steal them in these parts, as long as you load them out of here before the next moon. Soon, news will spread that the castle has occupants. The torchlights will carry far since it is so high on the promontory."

Alaric followed the captain below deck to calm the horses. Midnight Moon whinnied when he approached, so he moved over and patted his withers to calm him. "You did well on your first boat ride. And how did yer sweet mare do?"

He shifted over to untie Eli's horse, the mare clearly glad to see someone familiar, nudging him for a treat. He held out an apple he'd saved for her, expecting the journey to be a wee bit rough for the beast, but they needed horses more than anything. Maitland planned to bring more when he came on his next trip. Dyna's stallion was next to Midnight, but he was already calm.

Alaric led the three down the ramp and onto land, the animals pleased to be off the rocking vehicle. Eli ran over and wrapped her arms around her chestnut mare named Golden Gwyn, a name she'd given the young horse after her dear grandmother had passed on.

Once the three horses were settled, they tied what belongings they could to the animals and made their plans for the rest.

"Eli, can your mare handle the saddlebag and the bags with the seed inside? It is the most valuable. Derric, Maitland, and I can get what's in some of the crates onto our horses. Dyna, the dried meat and other foodstuffs should go first."

"Agreed," said Maitland. "I can get some of the weaponry. We cannot lose any of it."

Alaric and Derric moved two crates while Maitland paid the ferry captain, then the five of them moved along the path, hiding whatever they couldn't carry in the bushes when there was no one watching. There were a few around the dock, but they busied themselves with their work. Derric rode with Dyna while Eli and Alaric rode Midnight Moon, leaving Maitland to ride the mare.

It was midafternoon, so the village was quiet when they reached it. There were a few patrons at the tavern, though they stayed inside, watching, but not approaching.

Maitland said, "You and I will visit later, Alaric. When we return for the two locked crates, we can have an ale with the locals. Check out the supply store for anything we may need."

Alaric nodded. He couldn't help but wonder if they were being watched. The area was probably the most beautiful he'd ever seen, the landscape lush with greenery and berries, even in early summer.

Eli called out, "Puffins! Brigid always tells

me how cute they are." She pointed ahead and giggled at the colorful birds with the unusual beaks. Her cousins lived on Black Isle and loved to tell stories of the different wildlife near them. "Mayhap we'll see some dolphins."

Dyna pointed up at an eagle flying overhead. "Someday we shall explore just to see what we can hunt."

Derric said, "I'll be fishing for you, Diamond. Fresh fish is the best. I cannot wait to uncover the possibilities here. Sandor will love exploring. You do the hunting, and I'll fish."

After a short trek, Maitland led the group up the hill. "I was told otters and rabbits are plentiful, and red deer, especially near Ben More, in the center of the island. There are many otters along the coastline, but I've not eaten otter before. Any of you?" They all shook their heads in denial.

Derric said, "I've heard their pelts are mighty fine."

"We'll find out soon enough, I'm sure," Maitland replied. "We'll have much time to explore."

Dyna, always practical, said, "No exploring outside until we take care of the inside. We need to find out exactly what condition the castle is in. How long empty? How many creatures are living inside? You know how I feel about the sound of feet in the middle of the night. Other than our bairns, Derric." She shuddered, and Derric laughed.

"I'm sure there will only be a few squirrels, Diamond."

"I could only hope it will be squirrels. No rats, raccoons, or gigantic spiders."

Derric nuzzled her neck and said, "I'll protect you from the big bad creatures. Fear not."

The path was a bit overgrown but not badly. Alaric still couldn't shake the feeling they were being watched. It wouldn't surprise him, except he saw no sign of neighbors in the area once they left the town. When they reached the spot where the path to the castle jutted toward the water, he pointed to a row of deserted huts, no signs of active hearths or firepits anywhere.

Shortly after, they reached the front of the castle, and Maitland let out a low whistle. "That is quite a curtain wall. And the tower is huge. There will definitely be enough chambers for all of us." He led the way to the entrance through a gatehouse with a portcullis. Inside was a sizable courtyard built of stone.

Alaric couldn't believe his eyes. "Two stables? One of wood and one of stone. What luck we have!"

"Nice," Dyna mumbled, strolling over to open the door of the wooden stable. "Beautiful. At least ten stalls here."

Alaric dismounted and found his way to the protective curtain wall. "Maitland, the walls must be five times the thickness of Grant Castle."

"I have to agree, but being on the point as they are, they have to protect against the sea. I've not been witness to a storm at this level, but I've heard many tales. We will learn soon enough, but you can see the living quarters do not face the sea. I guess it was built in this manner for protection from the cold and salt water."

Dyna said, "Hurry up. Set everything on the steps and let's go inside. I wish to see what the keep and the tower look like. As you know, we'll be living here for a while, and I do not think the five of us can build any new chambers in short order. I cannot wait to see it."

Alaric said, "Do you need me to carry anything, Eli? We should take the seed packs inside to keep them dry. I'll find a metal box to store the bags. There are some in the crates."

"Nay, I'm fine. I wish to see it too. Hurry up, Maitland." They'd given him the honor of leading the group since they'd chosen Maitland and Dyna to be co-lairds while Alaric and Eli managed the guards and archers for any battles.

As a group, they climbed the steps leading to the keep, then waited as Maitland used the key they'd been given, opened the door, and peered inside. He glanced back over his shoulder and smiled.

Dyna pushed past him. "With that grin, I'm going in. Move aside, Menzie."

Alaric set his hand at the small of Eli's back and ushered her through the door, but he stopped as soon as his gaze settled on the great hall, just as Eli, Dyna, and Maitland had done in front of them.

Derric was on the far side of the hall at the hearth, calling to them. "There's still dry wood here! So much we won't have to cut for days."

Eli whispered, "Alaric, our new home is

beautiful. Look at the ornate work on the wood across the walls. The walls are mostly stone, but the woodwork is lovely."

Dyna nodded, but added, "A wee bit dirty, but just from lack of use. Not from pigs living here. Cobwebs and dust. Easy to fix. The mistress of the castle kept a clean home."

The great hall was long and majestic with massive hearths on each end. A long dais sat on the farthest wall between the hearths with lines of trestle tables to hold many clan members for meals. There was nothing of true value in the hall. If there had been, someone had stolen whatever they could, but there were tapestries on the wall, candle boxes, and plenty of tables, stools, benches, and chairs. A staircase led to a second-floor balcony with chambers over the passageway that led off to one side.

The hall was massive and made of dark wood and stone, the chairs and table on the dais adorned with ornate carvings.

"Chairs," Eli whispered since she'd been relegated to stools for the most part at Ramsay Castle. The elders sat in the chairs, not the youngest ones. "And I don't care if there are no cushions. I'll make my own."

Alaric hugged his wife, closed his eyes, and said, "Eli, we will have a wonderful life here. I'm sure we will grow to love the Isle of Mull."

He didn't let on that he was sure he'd seen someone hiding in the bushes as they approached. He'd find the fool later and send them on their way, though he'd been outside the curtain wall.

After all, Maitland carried the official papers from the King of Scotland.

This castle was theirs, and no one would take it away from them.

CHAPTER THREE

Tamsin

TAMSIN PEEKED OUT between her lashes, not wanting her evil husband to know she was awake. She'd lost their bairn, though they had no idea whether it was a lad or a lass. It hadn't been far enough along for the midwife to tell. This was a difficult event to process. She hadn't recognized the fact that she'd carried a bairn inside, hadn't felt it move yet. The midwife had guessed she was six moons along.

How had she not known?

She'd received no reaction from her husband. He'd locked her inside her chamber, sent Extilda in with a simple meal, but he said nothing. He usually wasn't that quiet about events, preferring to use his fists to add emphasis to his words.

In fact, she'd fallen asleep and awakened to find herself in her present situation, having no memory of how she'd gotten here.

She lay in the bottom of a galley ship, the waves rocking her, each movement shooting tendrils of pain through her body. Her resolve nearly broken, she didn't care if she ever saw her husband again.

The coldhearted bastard.

He'd sent their daughter to stay with his mother, without giving Tamsin the chance to give her a farewell hug. One more chance to take in her sweet scent, to inhale the breath of innocence that radiated from every moment of the wee lassie's year-and-a-half-long life.

Her cruel mother-in-law would kill the innocence in the sweet girl, something Tamsin had vowed to treat with such care that she would always have a beautiful outlook on life. It was not to be—not with a nasty father and his vindictive mother.

She'd always treated Tamsin as if she didn't deserve to eat the crumbs she dropped on the floor.

The ship slowed, so Tamsin closed her eyes again to make sure she could hear Raghnall's plans.

"Up there. On that rock. I will leave her there, see if she'll learn the lesson. Next time I wish for a son who lives. This one could not even live in her belly for the time necessary."

Raghnall had once been quite a handsome man, but he was turning to flab because he ate so much and spent his time ordering others to do all his work. His mousy brown hair had streaks of gray in it already. He didn't believe in washing his hair more than once a moon, something that repulsed Tamsin.

Had he no sense of smell?

He was taller than many, but not the tallest she'd ever seen, and at one time he'd been broad-shouldered from practicing his sword skills for battle, but no more. He shied away from doing anything that took much exertion. Thus, his belly softened, his shoulders shrunk, but his eyes, those dark eyes that carried such coldness, could intimidate anyone.

The man who commanded Raghnall's army of guards was known as Odart and traveled with him everywhere. Odart was the only man she'd ever seen question Raghnall and live to talk about it.

This time, his question even surprised her.

Odart glanced at his boss from the side. "You wish to leave her on the rock? She cannot swim, Raghnall. Or have you forgotten that high tide is coming soon?"

"I hope the bitch drowns. This way she will be forced to think about all the mistakes she's made. How she is not worthy of kissing my feet. She dared to give me a daughter and then a dead bairn. I'll tell everyone she went for a swim and drowned."

"Your pardon, friend. I've been with you for many years. I might suggest that you not put your fist to her belly if you'd like the babe to survive the next time. The midwife said if she'd kept him inside for another two moons, the babe would have lived."

"Perhaps it was not the wisest move, but a stronger woman would have protected the babe. I fault Tamsin, the lazy cow. If not for the gold I received, I would have never married her. She is too weak. Weak of mind, weak of nature. Leave her on the rock, and I vow to find myself a fierce wife, one who can swing a weapon and who will bring me many sons, not a bairn who cannot breathe. You know how difficult my life is, Odart, between my boss and my mother, the old witch. I cannot seem to make either of them happy."

"I understand, but Tamsin does not cause you any trouble."

"She does. Every day she doesn't give me a son, my mother complains at me. I'm tired of listening to her."

Tears dotted her lashes, but she forced herself to think of the vilest situation possible, anything to keep herself from crying. He did not deserve her tears.

Why had her sire chosen such a husband for her? There were so many men out there that she couldn't comprehend why he would marry her to such a cruel person.

She knew why, much as she tried to deny the truth. Her mother died when Tamsin was young, and she and her sister had always been a burden to her sire. They lived far into the Northern Highlands, and the weather could be brutal, especially to a child. He'd left the two lasses with his sister for many years, but even her aunt wished to be rid of her once she'd grown enough for men to stare at her.

Her father had sat her down and spoke honestly with her in one of his few moments when he wasn't befuddled with ale and whisky. "'Tis yer coloring, lassie. Yer hair is red, so red, like the shooting flames in the dark of night. But the worst part is your eyes. One blue, one green? They think ye are the devil sent by the fae. Too many colors."

Raghnall had said, "She's ugly enough, but I only need her to spread her legs. But it will cost you more because of the eyes."

So, her father doubled his bride price. The deal was made, and she hadn't seen her father or aunt again. And she had no idea what happened to her sister, Meg. She was only a year younger than Tamsin, so she couldn't help but wonder if she'd been forced to marry as well.

"Up there, Odart. On that rock that is its own island. No one will save her from there."

Odart's voice came out in a bit of a shriek. "That one? The small one?" Even her husband's second couldn't believe his cruelty if she were to judge by the tone of his voice alone. "But it's low tide. High tide will totally obliterate the rock."

She looked forward to getting away from the man.

"That is the one. The perfect spot for the bitch."

The man cast a quick glance back at her. "She's nearly dead now, Raghnall."

"Then let the sharks have her."

She said nothing, refusing to beg to stay with her husband. Losing the bairn had left her with little strength. The truth of it was that losing a bairn had saddened her in one respect, but there was a part of her that was relieved the child hadn't survived. Growing up around Raghnall Garvie and his mother was not pleasant. No child deserved that type of punishment. How she prayed that someday she and Alana would find themselves free of the Garvies, both of them.

She had to conserve what strength she had left, because if there was any way she could survive, she vowed to return for her daughter. Alana was the only light in her day.

She sucked in a deep breath as the vessel slowed, taking a quick moment to assess the damage done this time. Still sore from the fist to her belly, she dismissed this as something women dealt with often enough. She'd heal. The only part of it that concerned her was that she still bled. Was it usual to bleed so much after miscarrying a bairn? She had no idea.

Add to that quandary the tales she'd heard that sharks were drawn by blood.

She had a dagger hidden in the fold she'd sewn inside her gown, but she doubted it would do much to protect her from a hungry shark. Using it on her husband would be a waste of time. He'd only turn to use it on her—cut her face, slice her breast. He'd threatened to do both many times. Her ankle was swollen from the fall she'd taken when Raghnall had punched her. He'd only hit her face once, then delivered two quick blows to her belly. He'd yanked her by the arm and that had swollen quite a bit, but she didn't think it was broken.

She would survive. She had to for dear Alana. And once she had her, Tamsin would do whatever she could to please the man.

Anything to stop the beatings.

Chapter Four

Thane

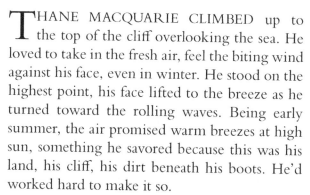

THANE MACQUARIE CLIMBED up to the top of the cliff overlooking the sea. He loved to take in the fresh air, feel the biting wind against his face, even in winter. He stood on the highest point, his face lifted to the breeze as he turned toward the rolling waves. Being early summer, the air promised warm breezes at high sun, something he savored because this was his land, his cliff, his dirt beneath his boots. He'd worked hard to make it so.

How he wished that witch of a mother could see him now—chieftain of his own clan.

He'd show her how much he loved it here. He'd been forced to come here nearly eight years ago, a fact that had infuriated him many times but had also given him purpose. He would right the wrong done to him and his two siblings. His daily task was to arrange for a way to find the cruel woman and show her how wrong she had been, but he just hadn't contrived a way to do it yet. His brother had told him he was afraid to find her.

On the contrary, he would rejoice when he found the bitch. In a way, his brother was right because if he ever saw her again, he'd probably kill her and be convicted of murder, his neck in a noose. That he could accept. To never be able to find her would be the worst, but he would prevail.

That someday would be soon. He could feel it in his bones.

His gaze narrowed at the ship that came into his line of sight. It was a small birlinn, bearing a sail and several oarsmen. But in the middle of the birlinn lay a bright object—much like the gown of a woman—though it was not moving.

Could it be a woman? They were not often seen on those types of vessels.

The boat sliced through the waves, finally slowing as it headed toward an area he knew held hidden rocks in high tide, but this was low tide. The rocks were in clear view, yet the ship headed straight for the outcroppings. Why? There was nothing there but three rocks, one flat enough to stand on, the other two pointed and unfit to hold anyone or anything. The only purpose they served was as an impediment to seamen in the dark of night, when the surface would reflect the moon with shimmers across waves, hiding the obstacles that could sink a ship.

The vessel maneuvered to go around the rocks, so Thane turned to head back to his castle, but his peripheral view caught something he didn't like.

Something he could not ignore.

The ship stopped next to the rocks.

He'd gone partway down the hill toward MacQuarie Castle, but he couldn't discount the slim possibility of impending malice about to take place in front of him. There had to be a reason the ship halted at that spot, as if it were arriving at its destination. For what? Then a scenario popped into his mind that he refused to believe. The woman was not moving. Was this all part of a plan?

He shook his head, his imagination getting carried away. They couldn't be leaving a dead body on a rock in the middle of the sea, could they? He turned around to stare again, his mind reeling, but it always returned to the same thought.

They wouldn't do it, would they?

Or would they?

He sat on a rock, vowing to see exactly what the ship was about before leaving. After all, it could be someone meant to spy on his clan or someone looking for a way to mount an attack against him. As chieftain of Clan MacQuarie, it was paramount that he do what he could to determine if this ship was preparing for an invasion. From their position, the sailors could see his castle clearly, watch the movement, decide if it was worth the effort. His castle was a long way away from most activity on Mull. He'd not been attacked since becoming chieftain four years ago, but it could happen.

No way in hell would he allow anyone to take away what he'd worked so hard for. After several years of living off the land in the forest, surviving on fish and rabbit meat, he and his loyal followers had finally found a deserted castle on the western end of the Isle of Mull and made it their own. His sister had made it better with her warm touches and her fine cooking, and he'd decided long ago that he would never give it up.

He liked his life.

Once he accomplished the one driving need in his life to find his mother for revenge, he would relax and convince his brother and sister to find spouses, then he'd spend his days hunting, fishing, and sword-playing. He was too close to achieving his objectives to let anything slip through his fingers.

He moved back, hoping he wasn't noticed, and found a tree to stand near to draw attention away from his large frame. Damn the gods in heaven, but once the boat stopped, one of the occupants bent over, lifted up the colorful blob, then deposited it on the rock before turning away and climbing back into their ship.

Had they actually disposed of a person on that rock?

A person in the middle of a sea that would cover and hide that rock within a few hours when high tide rolled in?

He ran his hand down his face as if he could pull back time and erase what just happened, but alas, the body was still there. After observing and studying the object, he made his decision about what he'd just witnessed. The man had deposited a woman on the rock.

The man settled in the boat, but another man stepped from the vessel to the flat rock, pulling his fist back and punching whatever they'd tossed there.

That movement convinced him he was right. And the fool had just punched a woman, a woman already down and not moving. He couldn't stop himself from bellowing, "Stop yer brutality, you spineless bastard!"

The dark-haired man jerked his head toward Thane but said nothing, instead jumping back into the ship and waving his arms for the oarsmen to begin their voyage back to wherever they came from.

Thane wished to stay so he could determine the fool's destination. Mull? Arran? Ulva? Where did the scum live?

That much would have to wait. As much as he'd vowed to focus on one thing only, his conscience wouldn't allow him to ignore the fact that an innocent lass had been left on an outcropping to die after being beaten first.

He headed down the hill toward their castle and the keep, shouting at the guards on the curtain wall. "Where is Brian?" Brian, his only brother, was his second-in-command and was often running practice sessions in the lists. They looked nearly identical, except Brian's hair was nearly black while Thane's was brown. Both extremely tall, they prided themselves on their physiques, practicing their sword skills as frequently as possible.

"He's with your sister in the hall," Artan, one of their top guards, replied.

"Artan, ready our smaller boat."

"Aye, Chief."

Thane rushed inside the hall, interrupting his siblings' conversation. "Brian, we've got to get over to the outcroppings."

Their sister Mora scowled. "What is wrong? Has something happened? Please tell me, Thane. You never get upset about anything, except… well…never mind. You never get upset."

"Some fool dropped a lass on the outcroppings. My guess is he beat her and left her there to die." Thane was certain it was done with the intent of murder, the inkling radiating from deep in his bones.

"Another of your gut feelings, Thane?" Brian drawled.

"Join me or stay behind. If you are too busy, I'll find someone else."

Brian, two years younger than Thane and two years older than Mora, barked, "I'm coming!"

Brian grabbed his sword near the entrance and sheathed it, following his brother out the door and into the stone courtyard, Mora directly behind them.

"Shall I come along?" she called out as her boot falls echoed across the bailey. "Who do you think it is? Are you sure it's a lass? What if it's a bairn? I'm sure you would need me to come along with you."

A chorus of "Nay!" came from the brothers.

"But I could help," Mora cried, chestnut hair

flying wild in the wind. "Surely, I could be of assistance. Could I hold her hand? Could I guide you when you get close to the rocks? Mayhap I should be the one to climb onto the rock?"

His sister definitely had the most pleasing looks of the three siblings, but she didn't care about her looks at all and refused to plait her hair. Perhaps that was why he adored her so much. She was not the typical lass found in the Highlands fussing over her gown and her ribbons, gushing over any man who was a possible suitor. He'd heard about those women, the kind who wouldn't attract him at all. Not that it mattered, as he'd vowed to never marry.

"Nay, Mora, I'm only taking the small boat, so there's not enough room for you," Thane said, stopping in his tracks. He knew how persistent she was. "There's only sufficient space for Artan, Brian, and me."

"Nay, it holds four or five. I can fit. I'll be quiet," she said, that look in her eyes he hated. "Can I sit in the middle? Or just in the back? Or anywhere else? Please, Thane?"

He did indeed have sympathy for his sister. Being the only female other than the housekeeper who visited daily was difficult for Mora, especially because he feared she had no role models. He did the best he could for her under the circumstances.

"Nay, we need room to fit another passenger, and I have no idea how large the person is. You will stay on the dock, Mora. Understood?" They made it to the place where the boats were hidden, various small vessels they had built and one large birlinn that could hold multiple oarsmen, kept locked not far from the coastline. Three other guards were already carrying the boat to the shoreline at Artan's instruction, something Thane was grateful to see. Artan anticipated Thane's every thought. An invaluable quality in the man in charge of the guards.

By family name, Brian was actually second-in-command to Thane, but Artan was more mature by ten years, so his insight was needed. Clan MacQuarie needed Artan.

Thane climbed into the boat, giving instructions as he readied the vessel. "Artan, you will lead us to that outcropping, the Trio of Fate as we've called it before." The group of rocks had been nicknamed such because their existence had ended the voyage of many boats while hidden during high tide. Those who sailed often knew every outcropping, but the younger seamen did not.

Mora stood on the dock, her hands on her slim hips. "May I come along? Please? I'm tiny, Thane. I can fit. Please allow me to feel a part of this rescue mission. You know I love to ride in any boat."

"Nay, not this voyage. Please make sure that Agnes is ready to care for someone, if I am correct. I believe it to be a lass who was beaten and left to die. We shall see. Be ready to help Agnes with her, Mora. Please do not disappoint me on this."

Mora stomped her foot and crossed her arms. "As you wish, brother dearest."

He hid his grin at the way his sister liked to pull on the end of her name for him for dramatic effect.

It would take a quarter hour to get to the outcropping, and high tide was yet a couple of hours away, but he did not wish to wait.

Brian climbed in, setting his weapon in the bottom of the boat. "Why are you suddenly so willing to help another, brother? It is not your nature and surely you know it." He arched a brow at him as he untied the rope that kept them from moving yet. "Shove off, Artan. Move along so I can be back for the midday meal."

"Do you ever think of anything but your belly, Brian?"

Brian spit over the edge of the ship as they pushed off.

"Disgusting!" Mora yelled, still tapping her foot on the dock as the boat slipped away from the coast. "I don't understand why I cannot go. How could you leave me here? Surely, there must be some way I can help. Come back, please?"

Brian spit again, landing in the water in front of her, a wide grin on his face. "Until later, Mora."

Thane couldn't help but wonder what the two of them would be like if they'd had their parents here to raise them. Would they have matured more? Matured quicker? He had to admit that they'd matured faster than many since he had served as both mother and father to them. Living in the wild for several years had made them grow up. Fortunately, they'd found a safe cave and made it their own. Three bairns alone in the wilderness.

Again, someday he would right that wrong.

He didn't have time to think on that at the moment. He would help guide the boat to the place where he had seen the girl deposited, then see if they could rescue the innocent woman. He prayed she was still alive.

But was she innocent? That he did not know.

Perhaps it was curiosity that drove him onward.

Brian reminded him, "You still have not told me why you care about this person. You know she's not a MacQuarie, so why the concern from someone who cares about naught but our clan?"

Thane couldn't argue that point. He shrugged. "I cannot answer for certain. I'll tell you when we get over there. I am driven to find out what happened. Call it curiosity from someone who stood on the point admiring the view before it was ruined."

Brian tipped his head as if confused by Thane's reply. "Or someone who was almost in the same situation eight years ago?"

Thane ignored his brother's comment. "It's my responsibility as clan chieftain to make sure that any ship in the area is not a threat. This clearly appeared to be an act of violence committed against an innocent person. It's my duty to find the truth of it."

Brian smirked.

"What the hell does that mean?"

"It means now I see the true motive of the journey. Not saving the person but wishing to find out who was behind the entire escapade. You have this voracious need to know everything and everyone around us. Let it go, Thane. The past doesn't matter."

It sure as hell mattered to him.

CHAPTER FIVE

Tamsin

T AMSIN COULD NO longer hide the fact that she was conscious. As soon as Odart lifted her out of the birlinn, she opened her eyes and whispered, "Please do not do this, Odart. I'll do whatever you wish. I just need to see my daughter."

Odart set her onto the rock, the cool water lapping over her legs on the lower end, causing her breath to hitch. It wasn't just cool, it was cold.

How long could she survive in the cold water? It was summer, but the water hadn't heated to a bearable temperature yet.

"You will send another boat for me, Odart?" she whispered. "Please?"

Raghnall's voice bellowed his opinion for all to hear. "I knew you were lying, wife. You always lie. You were awake all along. I knew it." He jumped off the boat and raced over to her, tugging her hair to lift her head from the rock before delivering two more blows, one to her face and the other to her midsection. "Next time, you will not burn my supper."

She recoiled from the blows, swallowing the bile that climbed up her throat. If she vomited on him, he would probably kill her. "Please, Raghnall. I'll be more careful."

"You are a worthless cow, Tamsin. You gave me a daughter when I demanded a son. And I've instructed you to carry again, with a lad this time, yet you are not strong enough to keep the bairn inside you. Burning the stew was the last straw. I'll not allow you to insult me any longer. You will stay here until I decide to return for you. See if I think you deserve another chance. Until then, think on how you can make up for all the errors you've done against me."

Raghnall climbed into the boat after tossing her back onto the rock, her elbow now bleeding from the scrapes across the rough surface. She wiped her hand across her mouth, not surprised to see blood there as well. How was she to get out of this mess?

How she wished her sire had never married her to this evil man. Were all men as vile as Raghnall?

As soon as he stepped onto the ship, his head jerked toward land as if seeing something for the first time. She had no idea what it was, but it upset him because he said something to Odart she couldn't understand and they shoved off, telling the oarsmen to go faster.

Had they seen someone on the coastline observing their evil deed?

"Hurry," her husband said to Odart. "Get the hell out of here."

"Who is it?"

"I don't know. Someone from Mull. I do not wish to be associated with this deed." Her husband dropped into the bottom of the ship as the oarsmen picked up speed, going back in the direction they had come.

Odart replied, "Then keep down. No one would know the oarsmen. Only you." He peered over his shoulder, scanning the area for any other fishing boats on the water.

Any witnesses. Tamsin knew Odart had a conscience, unlike her husband.

Odart continued to bark out orders, but Tamsin couldn't hear him. Perhaps it was because the rushing in her ears had become a loud intrusion that could not be ignored, borne from the sad truth that if high tide came quickly, her destiny could not be changed.

Her death would be due to drowning. The day had finally come when she regretted not learning how to swim.

But she had to do what she could to save herself. She bit her lip to keep from calling out as she pushed into a sitting position, stopping every few seconds to draw a deep breath to give her the strength to ignore the pain and continue.

Once she was upright, the water now reaching her waist, she looked toward shore, pleased to see a boat headed straight for her, ignoring her husband's ship that was nearly out of sight now.

She waved to let them know she was still here, that she needed their help.

Eventually, she would have to stand or the water would cover her face, so she did what she could to move into a vertical position. But each time she was nearly there, her foot slipped out from under her and she fell back, flailing from the fear of drowning.

She managed to get herself back up three times and opted to settle on her knees instead of trying to stand. It was enough to keep her head well above water and she could see the boat as it approached.

How had she reached this point in her life? Her mind traveled to the kinder days when she lived in a small cottage with her sister, her mother, and her father. Most of her time had been spent assisting her mother sewing and cooking while her sire left to hunt for the day. She'd loved every minute of the occasions when she and her sister had spent all day with the loving woman. She and Meg had learned how to cook, how to sew, and how to care for plants.

But the times with her father were not fond memories. An unhappy person by nature, she and her sister dreaded when her father would come home without any food, thus giving his hands and fists free range to swing and land on anything within his reach.

Tamsin preferred to go outside, even in the cold.

She'd thought married life would be an improvement, but she'd been wrong.

It seems the female lot in life was to serve as a way for men to deal with their anger and disappointment. They were to wait on them night and day, give in to all their needs, and then be there for them to take out their frustrations. Why did men hit so hard?

She hadn't learned how to handle her own frustration except to ignore it and pretend it didn't exist.

So, when she slipped and fell again, her head going completely underwater, she sputtered and fought to keep her head high enough so she could keep an eye on the vessel that could save her.

Unfortunately, the worst thing possible happened next. The vessel turned around and headed back to the Isle of Mull.

"Nay!" she cried out, knowing whatever she said didn't matter. It hadn't mattered to her father and now it didn't matter to her husband. She was doomed and it was time to accept it quietly. Perhaps heaven would be a better place for her.

CHAPTER SIX

Thane

THANE'S BOAT WAS nearly halfway to the outcroppings when he heard a loud splash from behind him. He spun around and cursed as loudly as he could. "Mora, horse's bollocks, but could you not do what you are told, for once?"

His sister dove beneath the water like a fine mermaid, then when she broke the surface, she tipped her head back and spewed a long fountain of water from her mouth.

"Shall we turn around, Thane?" Artan asked.

"If we do, the lass on the rocks will surely drown. She cannot stand on her own in the water," Brian said, pointing to her as she slipped and fell underwater again, arms and legs flailing until she got her head back above the surface.

"Mora can swim just fine," Artan said. "The lass cannot."

"Aye, but I do not believe Mora could swim all the way to the outcroppings." Thane turned to look at his sister, then at the lass sputtering behind him. There was plenty of time to get to

Mora before the lass would fall victim to the tide. He heard another splash and spun around just in time to see her flail again. And what if she fell off the rock? Surely, he would watch her drown before they could reach her.

He glanced at his sister and her solid strokes, then stared at the lass on the rocks.

"She's no relation to us," Brian muttered. "We have to get Mora first. You know it's our duty."

Thane nodded, knowing his brother was right. He had to choose.

"You are chieftain. You make the choice," Artan said.

Thane knew both men were right. He had to deal with his conscience. "Turn the boat around, pick up Mora, then come back for me."

"You? Where are you going?" Artan asked just as Thane dropped his weapon on the hull of the boat, removed his tunic, belt, and boots, and dove into the water.

Once he surfaced, he hollered back at them, "I'll keep her head above water."

Artan turned the boat around, and Mora yelled at Brian, "Hurry up. It's colder than I thought. I felt a fish on my feet, and I think it might bite me, and I want to go home."

"Then mayhap you should not have jumped in."

"Or mayhap you should have let me ride with you," she shouted, treading water and spitting toward Brian.

Thane grinned but held his chuckle inside, focusing his attention on the lass in front of him.

She noticed the boat had turned around; he could see it in her countenance. "I'm coming to help you," he called out to her.

She didn't see him. Despite still being five or six boat lengths away from her, he could detect the panic in her eyes. "I'm here! Here! I'll not leave you."

Her gaze finally caught him, and relief covered her face. The closer he came to her, the more he realized something that he hadn't given a thought to before.

The lass was beautiful. Even with her hair wet and tangled, she was a beauty unlike he'd seen in a long time. Red-haired with a pert nose, she depended on him to save her. He thought her eyes were blue, but he was too far away to be certain. Or did she have green eyes?

Then he noticed something else as he drew closer, his strong strokes cutting through the water as fast as he could because he feared she'd go under soon. He'd been right as he stood on the cliff.

The lass sported various bruises on her delicate face. A black eye, a bruised cheek, a cut lip were just the things he could see from a distance. Her gaze locked on his and she whispered, "Help me, please. I cannot hold myself up much longer."

She was weakening, probably from the stress of being tossed overboard, punched, and left to die by someone she knew.

"Stay strong. I'm coming."

She nodded, but he thought he detected tears mixing in with the splashes of water on her face.

If that were the case, then this woman was not as cold and heartless as his mother. He'd never seen her cry, and the bitch was his benchmark for judging other women.

"Who did this to you?" he called out. "Your husband?"

She nodded, but then tried to stand and fell backward, her entire body submerging.

The poor lass flailed wildly, clearly having never been in such a situation before. If she would extend her legs, she'd still be able to keep her head above water.

In her present situation, her panic would kill her.

"Put your feet down. Stand on your tiptoes. You can still touch the rock!"

If she would calm down, she'd be fine. But she wasn't listening, terror written all over her face.

CHAPTER SEVEN

Tamsin

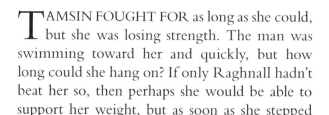

TAMSIN FOUGHT FOR as long as she could, but she was losing strength. The man was swimming toward her and quickly, but how long could she hang on? If only Raghnall hadn't beat her so, then perhaps she would be able to support her weight, but as soon as she stepped on her left ankle, it gave way and she collapsed.

She thought the man spoke to her, but his words were a jumble, the sound of the water hitting the rocks drowning out his words.

Under the water she went again, her arms reaching for anything to grab onto but found nothing. She held her breath, the battle within giving up to fatigue, to her fate.

And then an intense pain shot through her, the pain from her belly too strong to be ignored.

She thought of her sweet daughter, how innocent she was. How the wee lass loved with all her heart, always smiling, happily snuggling anyone. Alana was the only thing that made her fight. The thought of the poor girl being at the mercy of Raghnall and his mother made her kick as hard as she could to reach the surface again. Her foot found the rock to give her a place to propel herself up from, and her face broke through the surface of the cold seawater.

She gasped, clearing the water from her eyes and glancing about, shocked to see the man a short distance away.

"I have you. The boat will return for us, so do not panic. I'll keep your head above water. Try to calm down."

As he approached, she grabbed his arms, anything to keep herself safe.

His eyes locked on hers and he assured her, "Careful, now. I'll hold on to you, but you must trust me. You cannot pull me under or this won't work."

He stood on the rock, lifting her easily, his head well above water. He had to be a tall man. "Once we start swimming, you must allow me to hold you, and I'll keep you from drowning."

She nodded, giving in to his wishes. "Please don't leave me." She shivered, giving him the chance to grab on to her, to leverage his body in a way to keep her safe. He shoved off from the rock, and she fell against his powerful torso, his arm slipping around her neck to latch under the opposite arm, guiding her until she slid onto her back, leaning against him, his body keeping her afloat, something she'd never experienced before.

His voice stroked her soul as though he was caressing her skin. "That's right. Lean against me and I'll support you. Concentrate on keeping your eyes on the sky. Do not look anywhere else. Keep your head tipped back and you'll float with me."

Though it was difficult, she did as he asked, tipping her head and staring at the clouds overhead, her body taking on a buoyance she hadn't known possible.

A voice rang out from a distance. Another boat. "We have her, Thane."

She tensed immediately and his grip tightened. "Don't panic," he said. "It's only my brother. He's talking about my sister. Relax."

Tamsin did as he asked, slowing her breathing as they slid through the water. The man was huge, his body larger than hers in every way. His feet broke the surface way below where hers did, another testament to his height. The muscles in his upper arm rippled as he moved, the powerful waves not bothering him one bit.

"What island are you from?"

"Ulva."

"Your husband left you here?"

"Aye. For not giving him a son and burning his dinner."

"A surly bastard and a mean one too. What's your name?"

"Tamsin. My husband is Raghnall Garvie."

"Well, since you live on Ulva, we'll take you to the Isle of Mull, and you can live with our clan."

She tensed again. "Nay. My daughter. I must go back." She couldn't leave her with the cruel man and his coldhearted mother.

"First, you'll heal. Then you may return. You

need a healer if you hope to live to see your daughter again."

"Will you help me find a healer? And then help me get back to Ulva?" She didn't know how else to get back. She surely couldn't swim.

"I can't promise that, but I can promise to find you someone who will help you."

Tamsin relaxed. Even though she knew it was foolish, she had to go back. She wasn't even sure where her daughter was, but she had to see for herself.

Because she knew that if her husband was heartless enough to kill his wife, he'd do the same to their daughter.

CHAPTER EIGHT

Lennox MacVey

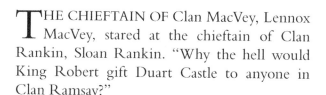

THE CHIEFTAIN OF Clan MacVey, Lennox MacVey, stared at the chieftain of Clan Rankin, Sloan Rankin. "Why the hell would King Robert gift Duart Castle to anyone in Clan Ramsay?"

"Because the MacDougalls didn't favor the Bruce. So, our king gifted it to the Ramsays."

"What know ye of the clan?" Lennox asked. He knew nothing of the Ramsays, probably because he'd been here on the Isle of Mull for too long. His sire had built their castle overlooking the Sound of Mull, and as Taskill, his only brother, was the younger of the two, the chieftainship would pass to Lennox and did the day his sire died two years ago.

He'd been off to Europe traveling and returned home immediately, but his experience was mostly in France and Spain. He knew little of the politics of the region.

His mother, Rut, paced behind the table, her long, plaited hair now gray from age. Her undergown was a stunning gold to match the gold and brown plaid overgown. He'd depended on his mother for most of his knowledge of running the clan—the numbers, the food stores, the boats, everything. But he was a quick learner. She knew something about nearly every clan in Scotland and the isles.

She didn't pause to explain, instead continuing her pacing. "Clan Ramsay is an honorable clan. They are known for one of the elders, Logan Ramsay, and his wife, Gwyneth. They both worked as spies for King Alexander many years ago. His wife was a renowned archer, as are most of the lasses of the clan. We could use some archers here, Lennox. We must befriend them, not antagonize them."

Lennox scoffed at the idea. "I'll stick with my sword skills and so will our guards."

Sloan said, "I don't know much more than that, but I'll gladly take archers to fight. I'd like to train as an archer myself. Have you visited yet? You are the closer one."

"Nay, but I had someone scout the area, and they have arrived. Three horses, three men, two women. It is said more are on their way. Two of their horses are warhorses." Lennox looked to Sloan for his reaction. "And they are beauties, so I was told." Sloan's arched brow was exactly what he'd expected.

They would all like warhorses.

The Isle of Mull was home to five clans that they were aware of. The MacDougalls, now the Ramsays, held Duart Castle in the northeast.

Clan Rankin occupied the northernmost corner of the isle. Clan MacVey sat between the Rankins and Duart Castle. There were two other clans on the isle, the MacQuaries to the west and the MacClanes to the south. Since there were mountains in the center of the island, they didn't often see either clan.

"Mayhap they'll rent a stallion out. I'd pay."

"We all would."

"When did they arrive?"

Sloan stared at the beams overhead, his brown hair hitting his collar and flipping up. It was Lennox's brother, Taskill, who all the ladies liked. He had the charisma that he and Sloan lacked. Lennox was the quickest in the group, but Sloan was a genius when it came to numbers. Unlike Sloan's brother, Rinaldo, who was not. His brother had a big heart, but they'd nearly lost him at birth, so his mother had said long ago.

Lennox knew his dark hair hadn't attracted many ladies. After all, he was seven and twenty and still unmarried. He had no immediate plans to marry, though his mother was often prompting him to find a wife, simply because he needed heirs to keep the castle in the family. Lennox wasn't in any rush.

His most attractive feature was his blue eyes. Some had called them cold as ice because they were a light blue. And he'd been called cold because he didn't talk much. Taskill did most of the talking for him, acting as his second-in-command. That pleased him. Lennox preferred to talk when it came to Sloan or his mother, or when the subject of the clan's welfare was upon them or growing his force of guards to protect the castle. For the day-to-day affairs of the clan, Taskill did the talking.

He'd heard the MacClanes hoped to overtake the entire isle someday, but with another clan to battle, that would be difficult. The entire conversation came to a halt when the door to Lennox's solar opened. Taskill stood there and said, "Visitors. A MacQuarie and a lass who has been beaten. They wish to see Doiron. What say you?"

Their mother pushed her way out the door. "I say get the healer. And I'll see to finding out who the bastard is that beat her."

Lennox followed his mother, Sloan and Taskill behind him.

He hadn't prepared for the sight in front of them. The lass wasn't just beaten.

The atrocity committed against her was done with the intent to kill. And by the look on everyone's faces, they all thought the same thing.

The poor lass couldn't walk.

Thane said, "We need the healer. She doesn't have much time left."

CHAPTER NINE

Thane

THANE COOLLY ASSESSED his allies. At least, he considered Clan MacVey and Clan Rankin as allies. He was often criticized for being cold and distant, but it was the truth.

Clan MacQuarie was a distance away from anywhere, since it was the western side of the isle. Alas, they didn't travel here often. But after one look at Tamsin, he knew he had to cross over and seek out the healer. Clan MacVey had one, something he was extremely jealous of.

Clan MacQuarie needed a healer of their own, but he had no idea who he could send to train or where. Doiron was getting on in age, so she was unlikely to travel. And the clan had few females, a precious commodity he didn't wish to risk losing to another clan.

"Follow me. I'll take you to her cottage," Lennox said, leading the way to a small hut in the farthest corner of the inner bailey.

The villagers did their best to hide their curiosity, but they all took in the state of the beautiful redheaded lass in his arms. He glared at each of them, forcing many to look away, but not before they got a good look at her.

Thane noticed that Tamsin was no longer awake. He wished to shake her, but she was not moving. He checked to make sure she was breathing regularly, and though her respirations were growing shallow, he could still see the slight rise and fall of her chest.

"Who is she, MacQuarie?"

"Her name is Tamsin. Her husband left her in the middle of Loch Tuath. Left her on a rock hoping when the tide rose, she'd die, is my guess, since she cannot swim."

Lennox jerked his head back to stare at Thane. "Who is her husband?"

"Raghnall Garvie. I know naught of him. Do you know him? She said they live on Ulva." Thane made a point to mind his own business.

Sloan began to cough. "Garvie? Did you say Raghnall Garvie?"

Thane shrugged. "I'll ask her if she lives."

Sloan glanced at Lennox and said, "Do not use my name when you tell anyone you saved her. He'll come for whomever saves her if his intent was death. Take my word for it. Evil bastard."

Thane snorted. "Obviously." He'd not be frightened by a cruel man. They were usually easily taken down, if one had the guards and weaponry to do so, something he needed more of, for certain.

They reached the cottage, and Lennox knocked

before opening the door. "Doiron, I have a patient for you. A poor lass needs your help."

Doiron came to the door, then peered at the lass, scowling. She had gray hair but kind eyes. Wide at the hip, she did not move quickly, but her eyes took in everything. "Any wounds? Animal bites? Anything like that? How long since she spoke last?"

"A couple of hours."

"Set her on the pallet there and turn your backs." Thane did as she asked, and the men turned away from her. Thane could hear as she whispered to Tamsin, then he heard the rustle of fabric followed by a sharp intake of the healer's breath.

Thane spun away quickly, shocked to see the bruises on Tamsin's body. He whipped his head back around as if he'd been burned. He'd seen men beaten that badly, but never a female. What the hell kind of man was Raghnall Garvie?

Doiron rustled again, then said, "You may turn around. I cannot help her."

Thane didn't have a healer, so he was more than confused. "Why not?"

Lennox said, "Truly, Doiron. You must be able to help her in some way."

"I cannot. She's been beaten worse than any man I've ever seen. I fix broken bones and stitch up wounds. I deliver bairns. I cannot help someone with no wound and no broken bone. You'll just have to leave her be and see if she comes out of it."

"There's naught we can do?" Thane scanned the hut, vials and tinctures everywhere. Surely there was something here that could help Tamsin heal.

Doiron shrugged. "Mayhap one other possibility."

"What? I'll do what I can," Thane said, unsure why he wished to see this through. Perhaps he should leave her here and return to his clan.

"I'm not sure, but there may be a different healer who could help this type of sickness."

He couldn't just leave her here, an odd force driving him to help her. "Tell me, please."

"I hear the new ones at Duart Castle are from Clan Ramsay. Lady Brenna Ramsay is the finest healer in all the mainland. I think one of the lasses is her granddaughter. It might be worth a try to see if she can help in any way."

"Have any of you visited yet?"

Lennox explained, "Nay, but my men have observed them. Only five are there and they do not appear hostile."

Thane thought for a moment. Surely, they would not attack a man searching for help. He had to do what he could. "All right. I'll take her there. Many thanks for your assistance."

"I'm sorry I could not help," Doiron said. "But I'd sure like to meet the nasty brute who did that to her."

Lennox, Sloan, and Thane all turned to look at her, surprised she was so vocal about it. "Why?" Lennox asked.

"Because I'd take him to the Ramsay archers.

I'm hoping one of the two Ramsay women at Duart Castle is an archer."

"Why?" Sloan asked, pursing his lips.

Doiron wore a smug smirk and crossed her arms. "If they are, surely you've heard of their reputation."

All three shook their heads. Thane had no idea what she spoke of.

Doiron chuckled. "The last man who messed with a Ramsay archer lass got an arrow straight to his bollocks. And she's not the first to do it. Her grandmother taught her. I heard he was fool enough to try to steal one of their young archers for a bride. It didn't end well for him. The lass's husband held him while she shot an arrow from afar." She pointed to an area of Thane's. "Got him right in his favorite parts. He did not survive. The others who came with him couldn't run away fast enough." Then she let out a hearty laugh. "How I wish I could have been a witness to that."

Lennox swallowed hard, Sloan moved behind Lennox, and Thane said, "He must have deserved it. I hope she's on Mull and she finds Garvie. It would be a pleasure to watch."

Thane moved over and lifted Tamsin from the pallet, but she made no sound and didn't move.

"Godspeed with ye, laddie, and with yer lassie." Doiron gave him a small pat on his shoulder as he made his way through the door.

He called back over his shoulder to her, "She's not my lass."

Doiron chuckled and tipped her head. "Are you sure about that?"

Thane frowned but couldn't think of an appropriate response. He'd never been more confused by anyone than he was by Tamsin Garvie. And since he viewed most women as useless, he couldn't reconcile what drew him to her.

He couldn't explain anything at the moment.

CHAPTER TEN

Eli and Alaric

ELI AND ALARIC worked on a section of fertile land to one side of the castle, but inside the castle wall, protected from animals and saltwater. They needed to get grains and vegetables planted. They searched the area and found a nice grove of apple trees, fortunately, and also found a grove of newly planted pear trees and berry bushes outside the wall.

They needed more than fruit and meat.

Maitland had gone back to the mainland to check on Maeve and to bring back more stores. He also planned to recruit a few guards if he could. One of their goals had been to see how many chambers they had and check out the stables and the cellars before they invited more to join them.

They were more than pleased with what they'd found. Though they were late in the planting process, they hoped to grow squash, turnips, and peas. Maitland would return with other supplies too. Hopefully, he would bring more seed, some wool for garments, and more kitchenware for cooking and eating. There was a small supply here, but if they had any visitors, they would not have enough utensils.

There were plenty of chambers on the second floor, and the tower held chambers as well. The stone stable had an extension they could use to place pallets for the guards to sleep in since it was close to the curtain wall. The wooden stable was closest to the gates and would be kept for the stallions because it was roomy and had good ventilation and storage.

The MacDougalls had built a beautiful castle.

Eli grabbed her belly and nearly wretched.

"What is it, Eli?" Alaric's face told her exactly how worried he was. Her husband was fully aware of her odd ability—the ability to feel someone else's pain.

"I feel as if I'm being punched in the belly several times. Do you see anyone around?" Bent over to protect her midsection, her gaze searched the area, making her way to the gate. "A stranger is approaching."

As soon as she stepped outside, she knew the problem. Two men on horseback were headed toward them, one carrying a lass who was either sleeping or unconscious. Once they were close enough to dismount, she could see the bruises on the woman's face.

An evil being had beaten her severely.

Alaric stepped in front of his wife and said, "Identify yourselves. What brings you to Duart Castle?"

The man who held the woman said, "I have a lass in need of your help. The healer at Clan MacVey sent me to you. Said she did not know what to do for her." He approached, holding the lass close.

"Your name? And is she your wife?" Alaric asked.

"I am Thane MacQuarie, chieftain of Clan MacQuarie on the west coast. This is my brother Brian. I found the lass near death on some rocks a distance from the coastline. And we do not know who she is, but she did speak to us after I rescued her from the rock in the middle of the water where her husband left her. She gave me her name then. We will not cause you any harm. We need help."

Alaric sheathed his sword and stepped back, allowing Eli to move forward to look at the lass. Eli took a quick glance, then asked, "Any wounds or broken bones?"

"Nay," Thane replied. "The MacVey healer said nay. Said she only handles bones, wounds, and bairns. We do not know why she doesn't awaken, but she was beaten by her husband."

"From what clan?" Alaric asked, his voice illustrating his annoyance.

Thane snorted and said, "Not our clan but one from Ulva. No one would dare beat their wife like this in my clan."

"Where is your clan again, Chief?" Alaric asked.

"We live in the west. You are new here. I was told you might have a good healer."

Eli nodded. "I was trained by Jennie Cameron and Brenna Ramsay. The best in all the land. Bring her inside, and I'll take a look at her." Eli was forever grateful that Aunt Jennie had been willing to train her. The need for a healer was paramount, and she'd always found the work interesting. Aunt Brenna had not been feeling the best, so Eli had gone to Cameron land instead to learn healer skills, closer to Alaric's family, which allowed him to visit with his brothers while she studied.

Aunt Jennie had prepared for Eli a leather bag filled with potions and ointments, linen squares, and special needles for sewing wounds. She'd already unpacked it, fortunately.

Brian stared at her, an odd expression on his face. "Are you one of those Ramsay archers they speak of?"

Eli couldn't hide her smile. She loved when their reputation as fine archers preceded them. "Aye, I am. But I am a good healer too. What know you of Ramsay women?"

Brian's hand moved to protect his private parts. "Just that you do fine work with your bows."

Eli didn't need to ask any more questions. Men were so foolish. She couldn't help but wonder how they'd heard all the way on Mull.

Alaric led them inside, pointed to a cot in a chamber off the hall to set the lass on, then motioned to the men. "I'll get you each an ale."

Brian followed Alaric back into the great hall, but the chieftain stayed.

Eli assessed the lass the way Aunt Jennie had taught her, then said, "How long ago did you find her?"

"Just after first light."

"Her bruises are still in their early stage. I suspect she is sleeping from exhaustion and pain. Will you ask my husband to find some goat's milk, please?"

Thane nodded and left.

Eli took advantage of the privacy to look at the girl's body underneath her clothing by stripping her and dressing her in a clean night rail. The poor girl was bruised from her thighs to her face, and the worst was in her belly. Then she noticed something else.

She was bleeding rather heavily between her legs. Had she delivered a bairn recently or was it her regular courses? Probing that area brought the woman's eyes open and she nearly screamed, but Eli caught her. "I'll not hurt you. I'm a healer. Did you recently have a bairn?"

"Nay. I lost the bairn."

That explained much. She was too weak was Eli's guess. Between the blood loss and the pain, she would need time to heal. Some liquid, some food, and rest to heal her bruises would be a great start. "What's your name?"

"Tamsin Garvie."

"Who did this to you, Tamsin?"

She let out a deep sigh, then replied, "My husband. I burned his dinner."

"Heartless fool. I'd like a few moments with

him. Is he here with you?" Eli put the bold question to her because it wouldn't be the first time someone lied about their identity.

"Nay. He returned to Ulva after leaving me on a rock in the sea to teach me a lesson."

"Or mayhap his intention was for you to die? Have you considered that possibility? Was he angry with you?"

"Aye. I left the pottage over the fire for too long, and I gave him a daughter instead of a son. Can you tell me how to make sure the next one is a lad? I don't know how to do that."

"Neither do I. Neither does anyone. It's God's nature to decide and no one will know until the baby decides to be born. Your husband is a fool." Eli leaned in to look closer at the beautiful lass. "Are your eyes different colors?"

"Aye, but I'm not a witch or anything. My sire had to pay extra to find me a husband."

Eli sat back, a little shocked. "Your sire paid your husband?"

"Aye, double."

"The husband is supposed to pay your father."

Tamsin looked confused, her eyes misting.

"Never mind." She patted Tamsin's hand. "That is no concern of mine. Tell me where your pains are."

"Other than the bruises, my left ankle hurts. I had trouble standing on it."

Eli checked her leg and said, "I'll put a wrap on it."

"Many thanks to you. Will I live?"

Eli nodded just as the door opened and Thane

returned with the goat's milk, Brian and Alaric behind him.

Thane noticed immediately. "You are awake?"

"Aye. I am thirsty and tired. Many thanks for saving me, my lord."

Eli helped her to drink the milk in sips.

Thane said, "We shall return in a couple of days. She can stay with you until then?"

Eli nodded. "Of course. She'll need time before she can travel again." Maitland and Derric had returned to the mainland, so it was just the three of them, but they hadn't uncovered any threats yet.

If she had the chance, she'd ask the chieftain why he was in such a hurry, and why he looked as if he wished to kill someone. She let him go for now, but she would learn all she could about this woman and the two men before they returned.

Something odd was going on. They had much to learn about their new clan and the Isle of Mull.

CHAPTER ELEVEN

Tamsin

TAMSIN AWAKENED THE next day, surprised to see that the sun was coming up and she was not in her own bed, but one she didn't recognize. Forcing herself to a sitting position, she rubbed her forehead, trying to recall the memory of last eve.

It finally came to her, the aches from various spots on her body reminding her of what had happened.

Raghnall had left her on a boulder to die, and a kind man had rescued her. He'd brought her here and then apparently left. She had memories of a young lass tending her, unlike the ancient healer they had on the Isle of Ulva. The woman was so old no one knew her true age.

The door opened and the lass she had met yesterday peeked her head inside, so Tamsin did her best to make herself presentable. She had to find out where she was and make her way back to her daughter.

"You are awake?" the healer asked.

Tamsin replied by nodding, waiting for her to enter. "Who are you?"

"My name is Elisant Ramsay. I am newly married to my husband, Alaric Grant. My clan was gifted this castle by King Robert, since it was unoccupied. We're going to establish a new clan here, Clan Grantham."

Tamsin shrugged because she was uncertain how to reply. She was clueless about King Robert, besides his name, and was oblivious to the Grants and Ramsays. It wasn't pertinent, so she didn't think on it much. "Where am I exactly? I must admit I'm confused."

"This is the Isle of Mull. You said your husband is on Ulva. True?"

"Aye. I've lived on Ulva ever since I married. I've never been on Mull before. How far away is Ulva?"

Eli came over and sat on a stool across from Tamsin. "I am new to the isles, so I'm not sure. But we'll help you in any way you wish. If you would prefer to stay here, you may do that too. But first you must heal. Since I removed your gown and put on the night rail, I saw all the bruises on your body, lass."

Tamsin pulled the neckline out so she could peek down at her chest and her belly. Eli was right. Even her legs were bruised. No wonder she was sore. She lifted her head and said, "Many thanks to you."

"How do you feel this morn, Tamsin?"

"I'm still sore. Hungry at the moment. May I eat something?"

"We have porridge. No honey yet. I'll get you some, along with goat's milk. In order to heal, you need to eat to get your strength back."

"I would like the porridge, if it is not too much trouble, please. And I will stay for a day or two, if that suits you. Then I must go home." Tamsin had to return to her dear daughter. First, she had to determine exactly where Alana was. She could be with Raghnall's mother, but that woman had little patience for a toddler. Where else would Raghnall send her? That was what she needed to uncover.

Eli got up from the stool and said, "We have the hearth going. Would you prefer to eat in our great hall where it is warm? We do have warm furs for your lap. I am the only one in the hall at present. I can assist you into the larger chair. There are small tables to set next to you."

"That sounds nice." Tamsin stood, pausing to gather her strength when she had to. The reality of what had happened hadn't really sunk in yet. The most important question she needed answered was about her husband's intentions. Why had Raghnall left her on that rock, knowing she couldn't swim?

She forced her mind to other thoughts, afraid to accept what was likely the truth of her situation. Her husband had wanted her dead and attempted to kill her.

Eli helped her out to the hall, and they made their way slowly to the chair near the hearth. The porridge smelled lovely, and Tamsin's belly reacted with a loud growl. "I am hungry. Forgive me."

"Naught to forgive. You needed your rest. Sit and eat. I'll keep you company for a wee bit."

The heat from the fireplace warmed her from head to toe and made her smile. "This is such a nice hall." Much nicer than any chamber in Raghnall's home. Much larger, much cleaner, much warmer.

"It is," Eli replied, assisting her to the chair and handing her a fur for her lap. "Once we receive all our supplies, I hope to have a nice rug for this area and some new tapestries for the walls. We've sent for cushions for the chairs. Once we dry some lavender, I hope the aroma will be pleasing too."

Eli settled Tamsin's food on the side table and then retrieved the goat's milk. Once Tamsin had taken a few bites of the porridge, Eli's questions began. Tamsin would answer what she could, but she needed to know who the man was who brought her here. She at least owed him her gratitude for swimming to her aid.

Eli said, "The man who brought you here said your husband left you on the boulder to die. Do you believe that to be true?"

Tamsin wasn't quite ready to answer that question, so she avoided it. "Who was that man? I must offer him my thanks. Is he outside?" Surprised to see how her hands shook, she continued to eat because she had one goal in mind: finding Alana.

"His name is Thane MacQuarie, chieftain of Clan MacQuarie. He lives on the western side of the isle, which is how he was able to see your husband's ship from the cliff near his home. He watched as your husband deposited you on the rock, striking you first."

Unable to look the healer in the eye, Tamsin took a bite of her porridge, then asked, "May I see him, please?"

"Thane returned to his clan. He told us everything he knew about you and your circumstances, but he is chieftain. He has obligations to tend to."

"What did he say?"

"That your husband intended to kill you." Eli was quite blunt, though her words did not surprise Tamsin.

There was no reason to keep the truth from her. "He did intend so. He failed because of Thane. He swam to me and kept me above water until a boat picked us up. Raghnall knew I couldn't swim, so he thought when the tide came in, I would die on the rocks."

"Was he angry with you for some reason? I know we discussed this last night, but I wish to hear your answers again. I fear you may have been delirious last eve. I wish to make sure I understand exactly what happened."

Tamsin had little memory of last eve other than knowing she survived because of a kind man. A handsome man, if she were asked. She didn't mind answering the gentle woman's questions. "Aye. I burned his dinner. The last straw, he called it. Dragged me down to the water and tossed me into the boat."

Eli chewed on her lip, so Tamsin took the opportunity to eat more porridge, amazed at how delicious the simple dish tasted. Somehow, she knew Eli was considering how to phrase her next inquiry.

After a few moments, Eli walked over to the hearth and leaned against the end of it, crossing her arms. "And I have another question for you. Were you carrying a bairn? Because you were bleeding when you came in."

Tamsin nodded, tears blurring her vision. "Aye. Raghnall was angry that I did not give him a son with our first bairn, so his fist went to my belly twice. I lost the bairn I was carrying. In fact, I didn't even know I was carrying yet. Then in the boat, he said it was my fault I didn't carry the babe until the end. Said his mother pronounced it a weak boy. So, his decision was that since I couldn't give him a strong son, I didn't deserve to live." She couldn't stop the tears this time, and she covered her face with her hands.

Eli moved over and hugged Tamsin. "Your husband is a nasty brute who doesn't deserve you. And his mother is a witchin' bitch. First of all, I doubt she could tell if it was a boy at that time. If he were my son, I'd cut off his bollocks."

Tamsin couldn't believe her ears, pushing back from Eli to stare at her. "What did you say?"

"I said he doesn't deserve you."

"Nay, after that." Had she talked about her husband's manhood?

"His mother is a bitch. But I'd cut off his bollocks. Or hit him there with an arrow. I've done it before, and it is oddly satisfying when the bastard deserved it."

"Your husband?"

Eli's eyes widened. "My husband? Nay, I adore my husband. He would never raise a hand to me or speak to me like that. You lost the bairn because Raghnall punched you in your belly. It is his fault the bairn died, not yours."

Tamsin heard so many odd concepts that she swiped at her tears to stare at her hostess. Did she speak truly? She again covered her face, shaking her head at all this information. But the most shocking part wasn't about her husband's manhood. She dropped her hands and asked, "You love your husband?"

"I do. I chose him. Did you not choose your husband?"

She shook her head, the odd words caught in her throat. When had she ever had a say in anything? "Nay. My father gave a large payment for me. He chose Raghnall. I never met him until our wedding day. You chose your husband? Your sire allowed you to have a say in your marriage?"

"Oh, lass. You have lived a terrible life. We live differently. Perhaps you should stay with us, not go back. Men respect women in our clan and treat them so. Beating is not allowed."

Tamsin had to admit that she had an odd pain in her head, and the thoughts spinning about were things she wished to save and contemplate. So odd compared to the life she knew, she had to give thoughtful consideration to everything Eli had just told her. Respect? Love? "I think I need to lie down. Many thanks for the porridge and the goat's milk, but I am overtired. Do you mind helping me back?" She couldn't listen to anything more Eli said.

Everything she'd heard upset her too much—so contrary to life as she knew it.

Could she live in such a way? It was too late to change some things about her existence. Her husband was Raghnall. His mother hated her. She'd lost her second bairn. Her husband had tried to kill her. And then there was the one good part that gave meaning to her soul—her daughter.

Now she just had to figure out how to change her life. But dear Alana was a part of her, and she needed her nearby. She'd have it no other way.

What the hell was she to do?

CHAPTER TWELVE

Thane

THANE MADE HIS way across the bridge to his castle, past the gates, waving to the guards on the wall. He glanced back at the moat, noticing the water was getting higher. That was a good thing.

He bellowed to one of the guards. "Stop pishing in the moat or I'll cut your rod right off."

"Sorry, Chief. It was an accident. I waited too long," the man answered with a grin.

"Mayhap you'll see your log floating down the way if you have another accident." Hell, but he hated to see men act like pigs. They'd all worked so hard to take care of this castle that he'd never allow them to destroy any part of it.

Even the moat.

"Pish in the forest or lose it, Bearnard."

"Aye, Chief!"

Bearnard was in charge of the men when he, Artan, and his brother were not around. Perhaps he needed to rethink this. As if reading his brother's mind, Brian said, "He does the job well whether he pishes in the moat or not."

Thane cast a sideways glance at Brian that let him know he still didn't appreciate people degrading their land. "We've worked too long and too hard."

His brother followed him to the stables, two stable lads rushing out to take care of their mounts, handling them while he dismounted, calming the beast the way they should. "I'll brush him down, Chief."

"Many thanks to you, Theo. Take good care of him. I hope to have a warhorse for you someday soon."

Mora must have seen them approaching because she came barreling down the steps from the keep, across the courtyard, waving her arms before she jumped on him to give him a big hug. "Where is she?"

He set her down so she could hug Brian. Then she swung back around to face Thane, chasing behind his long steps as he continued toward the keep.

"Tamsin. The lass in the water who nearly drowned. Is she coming along? Where does she live? Did she die?"

The villagers who had come inside to work stopped to listen, but he waved his arm to insist they move on and ignore their conversation. He knew that wouldn't happen, but he wanted them working, not gawking.

"We left her with the new healer in Duart Castle."

Mora began her usual barrage of questions. "Who is that? And who is at Duart Castle? What's her name? Where are they from? Who—"

He turned to her and took both her hands in his. "Mora, I promise to reveal all, but do your brothers a favor and find us a couple of meat pies. Lamb, beef, whatever you have. And bring me a goblet of ale or two into my solar, and then I'll tell all. It was a long journey."

Mora smiled and said, "Of course, Thane. I'll gladly get you some food. Cook just made berry tarts. Would you like one? Or mayhap two?"

"Nay, just the meat pie and a hunk of bread. Something not too stale yet."

Mora took off on a run as soon as he opened the door for her, then he stepped inside, Brian behind him. He hung his mantle on the peg by the door and left his sword in the stand nearby, his own stand he insisted to have for himself. He couldn't imagine handling anyone else's weapon. Plus, it prevented anyone else's hands from touching his beloved sword.

Brian followed him into his solar and sat at a chair on the other side of his desk, setting his feet up on a stool once he removed his boots.

"Are you comfortable now, Brian?"

"Aye, quite. That was a long trip you dragged me on, Thane. Two days nearly. We didn't need to stay so long. I don't know why you insisted on talking with the man who was leaving with his wagon of goods. How did he know they were there, anyway?"

"Because word travels fast on the Isle of Mull."

The door opened and Mora flew in, balancing a tray just so before whirling around to set it on the desk. "Four meat pies and a big hunk of the dark bread just dropped off here. Fresh. And it's delicious. Cook bought it from the traveling minstrel just this morn. Unusual, but he had extra bread. And I'm sure you will love it, Thane. It's the dark kind you prefer."

Thane's mouth watered as soon as his gaze fell on the fragrant meat pie and the chunk of bread. "You brought honey, Mora. Many thanks."

"Aye. I missed you both, Thane." She smiled, her innocence and bright outlook something he depended on every day. After the situation the three were left in many years ago, he often wondered how she could stay so positive, so happy, but he'd have it no other way.

His dear sister announced, "So I'm ready to hear all." She sat down and folded her hands in her lap, looking from one brother to the other. "I can be quiet so you may talk. Either of you or both of you. Who wishes to go first? I love to hear all that happens outside our clan."

"Not much to tell," Brian said before he took a big bite of the beef pie.

Her face fell, but then she turned to Thane. "Nay? Naught?"

Thane took two bites of his meat pie and closed his eyes to savor the taste before leaning back in his chair with a sigh of pleasure. "Brian may not have learned much, but I learned more than I expected."

Brian stood up and said, "What? What did you learn from that world of no ones?"

His brother loved to be dramatic, something else he depended on. If he wanted someone to stir up the villagers, Brian could do it and do it well.

"I visit and ask questions. Mora, will you allow me to tell you what I learned without interruption?" He took another bite and a sip of ale while he waited for her to accept what he asked.

"I'm ready, Thane," she declared with a wide smile and a nod.

"So, while you were napping in the stables, Brian, I had a chat with Alaric Grant. I also spoke with Eli and Dyna Grant, along with a merchant just leaving their castle."

Brian said, "Dyna Grant? I only saw one lass, and her name was Eli."

Thane grinned. "True. You were snoring when I found the lass in a meadow with an archery target set up on bundles of hay. Too bad because I've never seen any archer better than that woman. She made me think there might be a few women in this world worthy of getting to know, unlike many of the ones in my past."

Mora scowled. "We are not all like Mama or her petty friend Maidline either."

"You are right, Mora. I have complete respect for Eli Grant the healer, Dyna Grant the archer, and you. Three."

"And Tamsin," she announced with a scowl.

"Nay, I do not know her well enough to declare that. So may I continue?"

Mora hung her head and nodded. "Please continue."

"Clan Ramsay and Clan Grant ran a patrol to protect the Highlands from the English who were on a mission to kill as many Scots as they could. King Robert was in Ireland assisting his brother. Once that battle was won, he returned and awarded Duart Castle to the Ramsays to do as they wish. His anger with the MacDougalls has not changed, apparently.

"So, Clan Ramsay and its allies decided to send six of their people to manage Duart Castle under the name Clan Grantham. Eli Ramsay is newly married to Alaric Grant."

"Who the hell are the Ramsays and the Grants? Why did the MacVey healer know them?"

Brian's face had changed from boredom to curiosity. His brother never understood how important it was to search out information. They'd have never found Artan or their castle if Thane hadn't been one to talk with others. He pursued information the way his brother searched for the best meat pie.

"Alaric's grandsire is Alexander Grant and Elisant Ramsay's grandparents are Logan and Gwyneth Ramsay."

"Hellfire, truly? Even I have heard of Alexander Grant and his battle prowess. Did they bring warhorses?" Brian asked, wide-eyed.

"If you'd checked the animals in the stable besides sleeping in the one next to it, you would have seen one of the most beautiful black destriers I've ever seen. Midnight Moon was his name, and he was glorious. He pranced for me a wee bit, and I was duly impressed. And he snorted at me when I stepped near Dyna. Apparently, he's fond of both lasses. I've never seen a woman ride a warhorse."

"I've never seen a warhorse," Brian drawled. "I've only heard of them."

Mora shook her hands in front of her like she often did when she got upset. "Wait. You have not answered the question. Who are they? The Grants and the Ramsays. What did they do? Why do you know them? And how did you know they had warhorses?"

Thane brought the tone of his voice down to that calm tenor he often used for his sister. Living with mostly men had not been easy for her. "Alexander Grant and his brothers fought in the Battle of Largs, his huge warhorse dressed in chain mail. They have the finest horses of any clan, and he and his sons have been renowned as the finest swordsmen that live. Their horses can fight laterally, so its rider can swing on both sides, so they say."

"And the female? Who is she?"

Knowing how Mora ached for female kinship, he decided to tell her all he knew of the women he'd met. They were the kind of role models she needed to see, not the kind their mother had been for her. Ruthless, nasty, and selfish. Those were not the characteristics he would hope to see in his sister. Perhaps he would take Mora with him for the next visit to Clan Grantham. "Logan and Gwyneth Ramsay were spies for King Alexander before his death. Gwyneth Ramsay is known as the finest archer, even better than the men, and she's trained her daughters to be the same."

"Eli is one and Dyna? But you said she was a Grant."

"Eli is Gwyneth's granddaughter. Doiron knew that her aunts were the finest healers in the land. Can you believe our good fortune?"

Brian stared at Mora, who looked back at him. "Nay, please explain, Thane," Mora said.

"If we can become allies of Clan Grantham, we could learn archery, train someone to be a healer, train our guards to be better swordsmen, and pay for the use of the stallion. They have all the things our clan is lacking."

"Wonderful. What will I be?" Mora asked. "And what about Tamsin? Did she fix her? Will she come and live here? Will I have a new friend finally?"

Thane took two more bites of his meat pie before he spoke again, chewing slowly. He knew Mora would be disappointed. She was the only female who lived in the castle, though there were a couple who came to visit occasionally, but not exactly the kind his sister should befriend. All his guardsmen lived in the village down the path from the castle. Some were married with bairns, some were not.

"Tamsin stopped talking on our journey, Mora. She never awakened after we arrived at Clan MacVey. Doiron took a look at her, then came out and shook her head, said she'd never seen a lass beaten so badly. Said she couldn't help her since she had no wounds or broken bones. The poor lass was barely breathing by the time we reached Duart Castle. Eli said she hoped to help her, and she knew exactly what to do for her."

"What could she do?" Mora asked. "Did she save her? How long will it take?"

"I don't know. She said it would take a while for her to heal."

"What will you do now?" Mora asked. "Didn't you wish to take over Duart Castle? Do you plan to do that still? I think you should change your plans now. We should be friends, should we not?"

Brian said, "We'd hoped to take it over before anyone arrived. But we surely cannot jump into a sea of archers. We need to make our decision soon while there are only two women and one man there. Do you not agree, Thane? Once their reinforcements arrive, we'll not be able to attack at all. We must hurry."

"Nay, we are not attacking the Grants and Ramsays, Brian. Do not be a fool. If we did, their reinforcements would take it back. We do not have the soldiers to battle two huge clans like that, even if they are mostly on the mainland." He frowned, thinking on how this one development changed everything for him, and for his clan.

Mora said, "Good. Then we could become friends. They have lasses there. Are we going back to visit? Can I come along this time?"

Brian nodded. "Mayhap you are right, Thane. We could benefit from their existence and knowledge. Then how do we become allies with Clan Grantham?"

"And what about the man who hurt Tamsin?" Mora asked. "Will someone go after him? Or will you forget him and focus on Clan Grantham?"

Thane rubbed his hands together, because he knew everything had changed in a vein he hadn't anticipated. He would not even attempt to take over Duart Castle, especially since King Robert viewed it as his to assign. If Thane wished to expand his own clan, he had to give serious thought to what his new choices were, and this would take time. He would not rush this decision. "I haven't decided yet."

He had much to think on.

CHAPTER THIRTEEN

Tamsin

TAMSIN SLOWLY HEALED. She'd been at Duart Castle for three days. Finally able to move a bit, she assisted Dyna and Eli in the kitchen with the food since she'd cooked much for Raghnall.

She was more than surprised when the door opened one day and someone yelled just before three bairns and a group of travelers came inside, causing Eli and Dyna to squeal and scream with happiness, something Tamsin hadn't seen in a long time.

A very long time. It brought up memories of a sister she hadn't seen in years, someone she wished to see again, but Raghnall had denied her.

Once she had the pottage all set to cook, she made her way out into the great hall and found a chair to sit in, covering herself with the fur she'd used before. She watched the group in their joyous reunion.

But she couldn't take her eyes off the three wee ones.

Two lasses and a lad spent their time with Dyna Grant, their father behind them with an older lass. She watched the reunion, counting twelve new visitors plus the three bairns.

After a wee bit, one of the lasses wandered over to her, a small bow in her hand. "Who are you?" the white-haired lass asked.

Tamsin warmed up to her immediately because she reminded her of Alana. "My name is Tamsin. What is your name?"

"I'm Towa. I'm almost four winters. That is my sister Sylvi and my bwother Sandor and my auntie Astwa. And our papa. We came on a big ship. I'd never been on one before. Have you?"

"I have. Did you enjoy it?"

She nodded furiously. Her eyes wide. "It was fun."

"Do you know all the others?"

"They are all my fwends," she said with a fierce nod. "I'm happy to be back with Mama. Papa said we are to live here with Mama."

"And who is your mama?"

Tora pointed to Dyna Grant.

"You look just like her."

"My mama is pwetty."

"Who is the man laughing with Eli's husband?"

Tora turned around and watched, then replied, "He's my cousin Bwoc. He's going to be Alawic's second. My mama is the chief with Maitland. And I made new fwends. Hawk is from Black Isle and he bwought the ship. They will go back for more. He bwought some fwends with him, but I do not know them."

"What is your father's name?"

Tora scowled and said, "Papa."

Tamsin chuckled, something she hadn't done in a long time, and it freed her. The smile on her face was a swift reminder that the world could turn right again, if only she could get away from Raghnall.

Tora ran back to her mother and hugged her again, leaping into her arms with a burst of giggles.

There was so much going on in front of her that they paid Tamsin no mind. It gave her the time to study the group, something she enjoyed immensely because the atmosphere was so different from Clan Garvie.

In fact, she began to take note of the many differences:

How Dyna smiled at her husband, kissing him openly on the lips.

How Alaric always moved back to Eli's side, his hand frequently settling on the curve of her back. Raghnall's only touch was with the back of his hand or his fist.

How the three bairns raced across the hall with glee, only being spoken to when they neared the hearth, their mother shouting, "Away from the fire!" They instantly reacted, moving in the other direction. The three played well, only an occasional argument breaking out but quickly solved.

The biggest surprise to her were the smiles. She'd never been in an area where she'd seen so many people smiling. Maitland brought out wine to share while Alaric grabbed a pitcher of ale, setting it on the sideboard. Eli placed a platter of cheese, bread, and berries on the sideboard for people to grab as they chattered and eventually settled at trestle tables.

Tamsin daydreamed of a life without Raghnall, of a time when she could have a husband who smiled at her, bairns tugging on her skirt as they giggled and played while she managed the food and the stores.

Could she ever have such a life?

She doubted it, especially since Raghnall had control of their daughter. If she were ever free of him, had a way of finding her daughter, and found a new place to live and work, she'd never want another husband.

She hated relations and wanted no part of that ever again. The pain and humiliation were more than she could bear.

Nay, if she ever got away from Raghnall, she'd never marry again. She'd search out her sister instead.

She had to reason that she should be able to rid herself of the monster, since he'd already tried to kill her. If only she didn't have to return. If only she had her daughter by her side. If only she were completely healed.

But living with the Grants and Ramsays taught her one thing. It had only been a couple of days, but she witnessed a happiness in them that she hadn't experienced since she'd lost her mother.

Life could be worth living. One could live a happy life. But how could she do it as a grown woman married to a man like Raghnall?

If she could figure out how to get her daughter back, her heart could be happy.

Nothing else mattered to her. She had to heal and return for her daughter.

There was no other option.

CHAPTER FOURTEEN

Eli

ELI AND DYNA sat in front of the hearth later that night. Many had taken to their beds and the three men were outside checking on the horses. They'd brought two more stallions and three mares, bringing their total to eight. The stables could hold more, but Eli was pleased with the new additions.

Dyna sat back in her chair and sighed. "I'm so excited to have everyone here. And I'm thrilled to have my sister here too. I was not expecting to see Astra in the group. I'm surprised my mother allowed it." Astra was her only sister. She looked like her opposite because she had the dark hair of her father, but she had the same blue eyes as her mother and sister.

"You need someone to help watch your three wild ones. I love their enthusiasm for life. Don't change them. Astra will make sure they are just like you. Derric's skills can be used elsewhere. Any of the men they find to be guards from the isle will need to be trained. Derric is a good swordsman. He'll be wonderful with them." Eli wasn't ready to have any bairns yet, but when she was, she would ask Dyna for advice.

"At least with Astra here, I'm certain my parents will visit." She gave Eli one of her lopsided grins. "Getting a chieftain to leave their clan is difficult, but now that they are passing it on, Papa may come along someday."

"Probably not for a bit. I love visitors, but everyone knows we must get settled first. We've much to do, but it was too quiet with Maitland and Derric gone. This is better. We are nearly twenty now. It is an exciting development." Eli took another swig of wine. "I have a question I forgot to ask earlier with all the excitement, Dyna. Did you chat much with the traveling merchant? The one who brought the bread?"

"I did. He said there is a village a wee bit west of here where many worked for the MacDougalls. Said he was sure some would love to join the guards. I asked about a housekeeper. And a cook. He said there were probably a few who might be interested. He said he would pass the word that we were looking when he stopped at the village. With all these new arrivals, we definitely need someone to help serve, cook, clean. All of it. We have the coin." Dyna got up and grabbed the bottle of wine, pouring them both a bit more. "I'm so glad we found this in the cellar. It's lovely. What about the lass, Tamsin? Do you think she will stay?"

Eli's face fell because she'd taken a liking to the lass, but she didn't have much confidence that she would be with them much longer. Anyone who had to worry about being beaten like that needed to change their life, but that was a task not easily accomplished. "She's improving, but I'm quite sure that once she heals, she'll return to her husband because they have a daughter together. Her name is Alana, and she's not yet two. He took the child away from Tamsin. Said she couldn't see her again until she gave him a son."

Dyna bolted out of her seat and paced in a circle around the chairs. "Where did you say that bastard lives? I'd like to take aim at him. This is the part I don't like about starting a new clan. We always had hundreds of guards to call to our aid if necessary. Now we have few to help us. If we were on the mainland, I'd talk to my father about putting an end to that mean beast on the morrow."

"We just grew from five to nearly a score in a sennight. Be patient. Now that we have more than ten, I'm more comfortable leaving the castle in search of others—merchants, guards, anyone we can hire to help us grow and build our fortress. And Alaric has gone to town. Found out about some traveling merchants who will bring goods to us."

Dyna stopped and stared at Eli, planting her hands on her hips. "But I am quite serious." Her voice dropped to a whisper. "Where does Garvie live?"

"On the Isle of Ulva. Not far, but we'll need ships and oarsmen if we plan to attack him."

Eli looked at Dyna as a small smile crossed her

face. She'd seen that look before. Raghnall was not going to be pleased when Dyna finished with him.

Dyna said, "I have something to discuss with my co-laird on the morrow. You'll see."

Raghnall Garvie was in trouble.

Eli would get all the information she could from Tamsin.

Tamsin stepped back from the door where she'd been listening. She knew it was rude to eavesdrop, but she believed it was imperative to learn exactly how trustworthy these people were.

She loved what Dyna had said about Raghnall, but she didn't have the time to wait for Clan Grantham to find the oarsmen. Her daughter could be sold by then.

Her husband's mother tried to hide that part of her business, but Tamsin had heard enough talk about it. If they had wee ones who'd been orphaned, she preferred to sell them outright. There were ships from faraway lands who would stop and purchase any goods they had to sell.

Including bairns.

Would Dagga be that coldhearted? Would she sell her own granddaughter?

Tamsin would be gone on the morrow. She had no other option.

CHAPTER FIFTEEN

Thane

THANE STEPPED OUTSIDE his gates to greet the visitor he'd been summoned to meet, but he froze as soon as he saw who it was. He did his best to hide his shock, but he surely failed.

Tamsin stood in front of him, her hands kneading in her skirts, but she appeared completely different from the last time he saw her. She was one of the most beautiful lasses he'd ever met. Now that the bruises had nearly disappeared, her skin was flawless, her hair the color of his favorite red sky at night, and her eyes were different. One blue and one green, as he'd seen before, but now they reflected the sun, golden flecks in each eye.

He had trouble tearing his gaze from the lass.

Her words brought him out of his stupor. "My lord, I would ask your assistance to help me return to my home. I must make certain that my daughter is hale."

Artan had found her outside their gates,

surprised to see her alone, but there she stood, looking as lovely as anyone he'd ever met. Dressed in a new gown, she didn't look anything like the poor lass he pulled out of the sea. "How did you get here, Tamsin? Clan Grantham is a day's ride, at best."

"I hired someone from the next village to give me a ride. It was not the fastest horse, but I made it in a day. I did some cooking for Lady Grant, and she paid me in coin." Tamsin brushed the loose hairs back, her plait having been loosened by the winds of the isle.

"Come inside, Tamsin. Rest your legs. You may have healed, but you look fatigued. Have a bite to eat and we'll discuss it."

Tamsin nodded, allowing Thane to usher her in front of him as he followed her inside. Many of his men stared along the way, so he let out a whistle to remind them of their manners.

Brian came up behind him and whispered, "They do not see many, and surely not many who look like her."

"Doesn't excuse rudeness," Thane said between his teeth. Tamsin was far enough ahead at this point that he hoped she couldn't hear their conversation. Then he motioned for Brian to stay back and allow him inside the keep alone with Tamsin.

He knew his brother well enough to know he would interject himself eventually, but he wished a few moments alone with her.

Once inside, Thane gestured to a chair near

the hearth and motioned to a serving lass who joined them. "Two cups of broth, please, Agnes." She hurried away to do his bidding.

"You wish to travel alone?" he asked once Tamsin was settled. "Do you think that is wise?"

"I have a daughter I must see." Her hands sat folded in her lap, but he noticed that once she began speaking, she wiggled her thumbs, a tell that she was anxious. About him or the prospect of returning to her husband? He'd wait to ask that question.

He took a chair opposite and locked eyes with hers. Hellfire, but she was so stunning she nearly took his breath away. What the hell was wrong with her husband? "Do you not fear that your husband will do the same with you? He tried to kill you, Tamsin. I watched him from afar."

She whipped her head to the side, avoiding his scrutiny as tears misted her eyes, her chin lifted proudly. He was glad she wasn't totally intimidated by their discussion of her husband. "I don't know what else to do. If you have a suggestion, my lord …"

"Thane, please."

She nodded as she turned back to him. "Thane." She cleared her throat and said, "I owe you much gratitude for saving me. Many thanks to you." She sniffled and brushed hairs away from her face before lifting her gaze to meet his, something that had a powerful effect on him. "What should I do? My husband ignores our daughter, but he sent her away until I give him a son. I want my daughter. If I had my way, I would never return, but I cannot, in good conscience, leave the innocent lass to Raghnall and his evil mother."

"She's as evil as he is?"

"I think he learned from her. She often tells him what to do." She swiped the tears from her eyes. "I must find Alana."

"Did you ask anyone at Clan Grantham to assist you?"

"Nay." She paused and stared at her folded hands. "They are new, with many more just arriving to join them."

"Ah, you snuck away."

"They were wonderful to me, but they just had another group arrive to fill their clan—horses, foodstuffs, crates of weaponry, kitchen items, furs, linens, wine. They are busy settling their clan. They helped me heal, so I did not feel right to ask them for any more assistance."

He couldn't help himself. "More horses? How did they get them there?"

"They arrived in two ships, oarsmen from Black Isle assisting them. One boat returned, but the other is staying here."

Thane was surprised about the ship, though he shouldn't have been. He focused on the horses—he wanted a warhorse to breed with his mares. That would come soon enough, but how to help this woman find her daughter? He didn't know.

"Do you know exactly where your daughter is being held, Tamsin?"

"Nay. He hides her from me."

"You realize you may never find her. Ulva is a

large enough island with caves that he could hide her well."

Her voice cracked as she continued, "But I must find her. If you won't help me, then I'll teach myself to swim and swim across for her myself. I'll not leave her with that man and his mother!" Her voice came out a bit more powerful than she'd intended, and she flushed, a shade that nearly matched her red hair.

Thane lowered his voice in the hopes of calming the lass. "Allow me to think on it for a day, and I promise to help you in any way I can. This is not something that should be done without careful planning."

This seemed to placate her. "Many thanks to you." She gave him a soft smile and let out a deep sigh.

Hellfire if he didn't wish to hear that come from her lips after he brought her to her pleasure, then regained her composure while she lay wrapped in his arms.

The thought was vanquished with the burst of a door.

Brian stood there. "Raghnall Garvie is here asking for his wife."

CHAPTER SIXTEEN

Thane

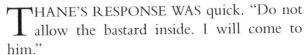

THANE'S RESPONSE WAS quick. "Do not allow the bastard inside. I will come to him."

Tamsin had bolted from her seat, frantically twisting her skirt, her thumbs wiggling again. Thane set his hand on her arm, hoping to calm her. "I'll handle it. Do not come out, or you will be giving in to his need for show. I will return in a wee bit to let you know how I handled the situation."

"Should I not come with you? He is looking for me."

"Nay," he replied a bit too sharply. "Unless you wish to be dragged out by your hair. I'll remind you that his intent was to kill you. I doubt that has changed." Then he spun around and followed his guard outside.

"Artan, the situation update, if you please?"

"Aye, Chief. He came on a small birlinn. Our men watched him approach. Four oarsmen, and he has two men with him. Each with a sword."

"Size?"

Artan arched a brow at his chieftain. "Men or swords?"

Thane snorted. "Appropriate question. Both."

"Raghnall is the type to be all talk, his two men are larger, beefier, more muscular. Her husband has no muscles that I can see. Soft in the belly, eats too much, talks incessantly about nothing. He carries no visible weapon. The other two have one sheathed sword each that are not as fine as ours. Easily taken, my guess."

Thane pulled on the bottom of his short beard, a habit he had when he entered into unexpected situations. He had a vague memory of scratching his chin when he was young, and an older man, he guessed his sire, would slap his hand away, telling him not to be indecisive.

This was his small form of rebellion. The man did not deserve the title of father. He left the three siblings long ago with their harsh mother, who deserted them not long after.

Neither one deserved bairns. Both were the reason he would never have any of his own.

He scratched his neck beneath his beard, an act of defiance he didn't deny himself. It did lessen his anger to a low simmer, so he didn't stop it. He was actually looking forward to looking the man in the eye.

He strode through the gates and across the bridge, marching up to Tamsin's husband, because he knew exactly which one he was, thanks to Artan's thorough description.

Stopping directly in front of the man who

backed up one step, he looked down at him with derision. "You are Raghnall Garvie?"

"Aye. Who the hell are you?"

He pulled his fist back and landed a hard blow on the man's cheekbone, nearly knocking him off his feet. Both his guards attempted to grab Thane, one placing a dagger at his throat, but Thane took the dagger from him with one smooth move. He drove the flat of his hand into the swine's chin, snapping his head back and sending him to the ground.

The third man dropped his weapon and held up his hands, stepping back.

Raghnall rubbed his cheek and said, "What the hell was that for?"

Thane's hands went to his hips, where he liked to keep them in case he had to unsheathe his weapon quickly. "For trying to kill an innocent lass."

"Innocent? The wee bitch is far from innocent. She burned my dinner among many other offenses." Raghnall didn't reach for his weapon, but the fury in his eyes made Thane wonder how Tamsin had survived living with this arrogant fool. "She is to give me a son, and she can't even do that. The one thing a woman is expected to do for her husband, and she's failed."

"Then why do you want her back if she displeases you so?"

"Because she belongs to me. I was told you brought her to your castle. I left her on the rock to think on her failures. I would have retrieved her."

"Before the tide came up?" Thane drawled.

"Aye. Return her to me. I own her."

Thane took a step closer, lowering his voice, one of his favorite tactics to get his point across. He found yelling to be a waste of time. "And did punching the lass before you left her in the middle of the loch to 'think on her failures' make you feel like a strong man? Did it make you feel powerful to beat someone who has no chance of fighting back?"

The fury increased in Garvie's eyes, but he hadn't moved. Thane watched for any twitch in the man's demeanor that would give away his next step.

"She's my wife, and I'll do with her what I please. Return her to me."

"So, you can beat her again? Do you think your dick will grow if you beat a woman? Is that why men with small penises like you beat women?"

Garvie lost it, reaching for his paltry weapon, but Thane was faster, taking a step back and withdrawing his sword, the point at Garvie's throat before the man could raise his dagger.

Lazy arse that Garvie was, Thane was not going to kill him yet. "You live on Ulva?"

"I own Ulva."

Thane laughed at this boast because he knew it wasn't true, but the man was full of lies. Evil ran thick in his veins.

Brian and Artan both stood in front of Garvie's men with their weapons drawn to keep them from interfering.

Thane continued, "Get off my land. Take yer

arse back to Ulva and keep it there or I'll slice your neck right now."

He pushed the point in, drawing blood, but not too much. Garvie paled.

"I'll go with him!" Tamsin's voice carried from the bridge, if he were to guess. "Do not kill him, my lord. I will return. I've caused you enough trouble."

Thane pulled his weapon back and Garvie rubbed his neck, wiping the blood on his tunic. Garvie shouted, "Answer me this first, wife. Did you whore for him?"

Another fist shot out so fast, Garvie never saw it coming. Thane couldn't help himself. How could he treat a lass as beautiful as Tamsin the way he was? Burning his dinner was hardly a crime punishable by death.

"I did not touch your wife except to get her to a healer." Then he turned to Tamsin and said, "I would advise against going with him. You know he'll beat you again."

Garvie looked at his wife, the hatred for her evident in his face. "If you wish to see Alana again, wife, get your arse in the boat. Otherwise, I'll send her bones to you."

Tamsin ran down the bank toward the boat. Before climbing in, she turned back to Thane and gave him a small bow of thanks.

Thane wished to beat the smug look from Garvie's face, but he kept his hands to his side as the fool turned around and headed back to the vessel.

He was nearly at the ship when Thane couldn't

stop himself from calling out, "You have not seen the last of me, Garvie."

Garvie retorted, "Oh, you can count on seeing me again, and next time I'll be in control, not you. I'll have you drawn and quartered on Ulva if you dare to come for her."

Thane had the odd feeling he'd just been given a dare he had to meet. But another part of him knew the truth of the situation and hoped Tamsin would survive long enough to locate her daughter.

The birlinn left shore, and Thane turned around, knowing it would be best if he didn't watch Tamsin.

Instead, he headed back across the bridge, just now noticing that every person in his clan stood outside the curtain wall or on it, watching the show. A small round of applause started. It was something he'd never heard before.

Mora ran at him, launching herself and throwing her arms around her big brother. "Thane, you were wonderful. Thank you for trying to protect her, but she must do what her heart tells her. Even if she is foolish."

He gave his sister a squeeze and then set her down, striding through the gates and into the courtyard while the others all returned to their work. He'd never felt so powerless.

That was untrue. The time he'd felt the worst in his life was when his own mother had instructed a man to throw the three of them on a ship and leave them on an island somewhere far away.

And he had naught but a dagger to take care

of himself and his brother and sister. When they stood on the rocky coastline with one sack of belongings as they watched the birlinn depart, then he'd felt powerless.

The surprise was that he and his siblings were stronger than he would have ever guessed. How he wished their mother could see them now. Someday, he'd show her. He'd prove to her how wrong she was to leave them to die.

But it had been a challenge, something that had humbled and given Thane the drive to be the best he could be.

Brian, Mora, and Artan followed him inside the keep, straight into his solar. "What are you going to do about it, Thane?" Brian asked.

"I've got to think on it."

Artan said, "May I offer a suggestion?"

Once they were seated in the solar, the door closed, Thane nodded to the leader of his guard. "Go ahead, Artan." He trusted the man because he used common sense and strategy instead of emotion, which Brian used too often. Artan also knew the isle much better than Thane did.

"Since you are no longer interested in capturing Duart Castle …"

"Because we couldn't. It's an impossibility in view of the new inhabitants. According to Tamsin, another dozen people have arrived to fill their chambers. Finish your thought, please. Forgive my interruption."

"Then may I suggest taking over Garvie's castle on Ulva? He claims to own the isle, which I don't believe, but how many inhabit the isle? It is so close to us, yet we know naught about it."

Thane leaned back and steepled his fingers in front of him, his elbows resting on the arms of his chair. Artan had made a good suggestion, and Thane would give him credit for it, even though he'd been considering the same objective. If he wished to build Clan MacQuarie, he needed to take on land somewhere, and Ulva was one of the closest isles.

"The isle is close and small."

Brian seemed bothered, his head shaking. "But why an island? Why not land close to us?"

Thane considered Brian's questions, giving him confirmation on his thoughts about his brother. Just two years younger than Thane's nine and ten, his thoughts never demonstrated any true understanding of his actions and the possible repercussions. His suggestions were often instantaneous, showing no real thought to the consequences of his plans.

"Brian, there is no land that has been inhabited close to us. You know this. Forests, rugged coastline. We need land where we can plant and harvest our food. We cannot subsist on meat and fish alone. We need grains and vegetables. A place to plant more fruit trees. When your number grows larger, you must have food to fill the bellies. I'd like sheep from the mainland for the wool. Highland cattle. Warhorses. A field to sow our beans and oats. We need so much more."

"And lasses," Brian said, avoiding Thane's gaze on this one. "You know we need lasses, Thane.

They are not all like Mama. I'd like to marry someday."

Thane had heard this from many of his men. Perhaps it was time for him to reconsider. They'd never survive without bairns. It was a fact he could no longer deny. "I've been considering your thoughts, Brian. But give me more time to think on it. Beyond the lasses, Ulva is a better consideration because I believe they have been there long enough to live off the land. But this is something else we need to study before I decide."

"You've considered it already, have you not, Chief?" Artan asked.

"I have, but I'm pleased to hear you believe it to be a wise consideration. I'll agree to researching the possibility, but first we must discover how many guards he can mobilize and how many other large groups are on the isle. Are there fertile fields on the isle? That's where I would start, Artan. Research, then we'll gather the information and consider where to go from there."

Mora did that little wiggle she did when a new idea popped into her head, the wiggle lasting for as long as she had to hold it inside. "What is it, Mora?"

She clapped her hands and stood. "While you are there, please check on Tamsin. I think you should marry her, Thane," Mora said with a grin. "She's beautiful. Do you not agree? Do you not think you should have an heir? Would you not like some bairns? I'd like to be an auntie."

"Tamsin is married, Mora, or have you forgotten this?"

Brian chuckled. "Not if you rid the world of the evil bastard. Besides, he tried to kill her. That should serve as a reason for her not to be required to serve as his wife any longer."

"I agree she is a beauty, but I'll not be marrying Tamsin or anyone else. You know why, Mora."

Brian's face lit up. "Then you'll not mind if I go after her? If you decide to save her, I'll have her, brother. She is a fine beauty."

Thane did something without even thinking on it. He shot up from his chair and gave his desk a shove toward his brother, not hitting him but coming close enough for Brian to jump out of his chair. "You cannot have her, Brian."

No one said anything until Mora wrinkled her nose and whispered, "He likes her." Then she nodded and waggled her brow.

Thane couldn't deny her supposition. Damn it all to hell and back, but she was speaking a truth. He'd never admit it, especially because they both knew he held a certain belief, a certain rule in his life, that wouldn't allow such a possibility.

Other than his sister, he hated women. Then how had he allowed this unlikely event, this mysterious but browbeaten woman, to crack his granite heart?

He was drawn to Tamsin. But he didn't like it one bit.

CHAPTER SEVENTEEN

Tamsin

TAMSIN SAT IN her chamber, shivering because there was no firewood to burn. She wrapped a thin fur around her, but it didn't help much.

The ride back from Mull had been uneventful, since her husband spent all his time talking with the guards about what a fine job they'd done retrieving her. They were all lies from her vantage point, but she'd not said a word. He had a way of twisting everything to make himself look like the most powerful man in the world.

The only event that involved her was when he turned and spit in her lap. Tamsin thought she would heave over the side of the ship. The man was vile.

But she would mind her manners because she knew he pushed her, looking for any excuse to beat her. He didn't often beat her in front of others, preferring to do so in private, especially without a valid reason, and he was hoping she would give him that reason, but she refused. She anticipated his hand would be ready to strike her at any indiscretion she committed, so she sat still and acted as though nothing was wrong.

She would wait until they were alone to ask about Alana.

In fact, her mind was already planning the best way to go about learning the location of her daughter. There was one serving lass she trusted, so she thought to ask her where Alana was being held. Asking her husband would be a waste of her time and would probably provoke a litany of lectures and slaps. Raghnall would never reveal the truth unless he had a reason that would benefit himself.

In view of the situation at hand, she had to wait to see how to approach him.

But she vowed to find Alana. She had to know she was hale and safe.

She decided the best thing to do with her time was to make a plan, find a way to get away from Raghnall, uncover where her daughter was being kept, and then concoct a way to get her off the isle.

There were numerous regrets about her trip to the Isle of Mull. She should have asked someone like Eli to teach her how to swim. She wished she'd learned how to use a bow and arrow, though she'd never seen either around Raghnall's home, and she knew he would never have allowed her to bring weaponry along.

Tamsin was all alone on the Isle of Ulva. How would she ever find her way off the isle? And if she found a way for herself, how could she manage to get Alana away when she had no idea where the child was hidden?

Raghnall lived in a type of longhouse much like the Norse lived in. That was what her mother always called these structures. Her mother-in-law wasn't far away, residing in a separate but similar building, but Tamsin didn't know which one. There were three buildings behind their main longhouse. But there were only two ways to locate her daughter.

She would ask Alma, the only serving lass to ever be kind to her, if she knew where Alana was. If the serving lass couldn't help her, then the only alternative was Raghnall.

Knowing that her ultimate goal was to find her daughter, Tamsin accepted the sad fact that since Raghnall had kept her isolated ever since their marriage, she had no friends to help her.

Forcing herself out of her chair, she moved about the chamber, rubbing her arms for warmth. The chamber was cold, even in the early summer months. The sun was never upon her window, the trees behind the house preventing the warmth she needed from the golden orb in the sky.

The door banged open with a force unlike she'd ever seen before, and her husband filled the doorway. "Are you prepared to give me a son? I will plant my seed again, but it is up to you to guarantee that this bairn is a lad. Do you agree, wife?"

She had no other choice but to do what he said, even though she had no idea how to accomplish such a thing. She knew what she had to endure to make a child, but how to make sure it was a boy was something she'd never learned.

"Ready yourself." He stepped out and said, "I will return quickly."

She had no choice in this matter. He was the only path to Alana.

CHAPTER EIGHTEEN

Thane

THANE RODE WITH Mora, Brian, Artan, and two other guards to Duart Castle. Mora was so excited she could hardly contain herself. Thank the lord above for his sister. Her enthusiasm and outlook on life always made him smile.

He hated to admit to anyone why she was the only female who lived inside the walls of his castle, but he also couldn't change it. The belief lived inside him with a force he still couldn't fight.

His own mother had treated them so poorly that he didn't trust any female. Only his sister. And when those evil memories forced their way into his mind, he had to fight to quash them back where he'd never think on them again.

The memories were too painful.

This trip often brought past memories to the forefront of his mind, though he had no idea why. They had to go around the mountain, through the forests, to a high point that was a favorite of anyone who traveled across the isle because the view was unbelievable. He always stopped to look in all four directions, toward the Firth of Lorne, Loch Linnhe, the Sound of Mull. One could see forever.

He held his hand up to stop their progression, making a motion to his brother to occupy Mora while he dismounted and wandered off the path a bit. "I'll return in a few moments, Mora." They were accustomed to his penchant for stopping at this point.

He faced the Sound of Mull, memories of times as a child racing though his mind. If he could only stop them so he could study each one. Visions of sitting a horse with his father, a time of happiness and safety. He could almost hear the rumble of his sire's voice as he instructed another man with them, though Thane ignored the man, so excited for their journey that he could barely keep still. His father's hand would often rub his arm or pat his leg, those small motions of affection something he treasured. He'd taken Thane to a cave that day, one they'd explored for a long while. His father searched for something, but he never knew what it was he'd hoped to find.

The vision bothered him because it didn't fit with the image of a man who would have deserted three bairns and their mother, something their mother reminded them of often.

The second memory was the one that haunted him more. It was of a woman he didn't know grabbing Mora while his father bellowed at him. "Run, Thane. Take Brian with you into the forest!" A rainstorm pelted them, but he took Brian's hand and ran, looking back to see where Mora and his father was. When he turned around, he stared at the rivers of blood running by his feet. In the distance, the sea was visible in every direction. That was all he recalled.

But from each memory, he attempted to retrieve another bit of information that could prove important. Who was the woman? It was not their mother because this person was too pleasant. He'd decided it must have been an aunt, possibly a sister to his father.

But where had the blood come from?

And the last words he'd heard, he would never forget. "Thane, take care of Brian and Mora!"

He had no other memory than that. His age must have been around five summers, while Brian would have been three and Mora just a year. They had no memories at all from those times, so he had no help in the matter.

But the memories haunted him whenever he crossed the isle and sometimes in his dreams. He would awaken in a cold sweat. "Thane, are you hale?"

His sister's voice often took him from his memories, but he was glad of it this time. "I'm fine, Mora. Just admiring the view. We can move on."

"It is the best view of all. Even better than the view from our battlements. Do you not agree? What do you think, Brian? Do you think they'll allow me to look out over the battlements at Duart Castle? Do you think they will like me, Thane?"

He smiled; the memories gone for now. "I think Lady Ramsay and Lady Grant will both love you, Mora. Who wouldn't love my sister?" He meant that statement with every beat of his heart. She was a blessing to all of them. "All you need to do is ask, and I think they'll honor your request to look over the battlements. I'd like to join you as I'm sure it is quite a view."

"May I visit the warhorses with you? Could I visit their kitchens too? Will you ask if she will teach me how to shoot an arrow?"

"Aye, aye, and we'll see about the archery. Mora, do not expect too much. I will probably visit with the men more than the women on this trip."

"But surely the mistress will allow me to visit inside the great hall. I would love to see how they have decorated it. Do they have tapestries? Or plaids? Or do they use flora and pines to decorate? What do they cook the most? How many cooks do they have? I have so many questions."

Thane nearly rolled his eyes at his sister's curiosity, but he was used to it by now. It was part of who she was, and he accepted it. "I promise to introduce you to Eli, and you may ask her whatever you wish, but will you promise to ask her only one question at a time?"

"I promise." Mora scowled before she gave him the most honest answer she could. "I'll try my best."

"That's all I can ask." He treasured her honesty, something he could always count on. Those small treasures were few and far between.

They noticed the change in the air, the proximity to the sea always the first sign of the nearby coastline. In the distance, the castle sat high near Duart Point. It was an imposing structure, quite solid with a thick curtain wall to protect it from not just invaders but also the elements. Thane had as many questions as Mora.

Along the way, he thought again about Artan's ideas surrounding Ulva and Raghnall Garvie. Their next visit would be to the isle. There was a narrow area where one could use a small boat to traverse the loch. Many crossed at that point, and he thought there might be a boat for hire to take beyond, a vessel that would carry more people. He thought to check into that.

He could take their ship or a small boat, but since he didn't trust Garvie and his men, he had a fear that the ship would be missing when they returned. The man was a thief through and through. Thief and a liar, if Thane were to wager.

When they approached the castle, he made his way to the gates, surprised to see a group of villagers waiting outside for admittance.

Brian glanced over at him. "What do we do?"

Thane approached, making his way through the villagers, taking the reins of Mora's horse and leading her straight to the gatehouse. "Thane MacQuarie to see Eli and Alaric Grant, if you please."

"Just one moment," the guard said, leaving

and returning quickly. "You may enter. My lady Elisant will meet you on the steps to the keep."

"Many thanks to you," he said, waving to his guards and the others to follow him in once the gate opened.

Inside, a tall, bearded man stood and directed them to the stables, taking Mora's horse first. "The name is Maitland Menzie. We're hiring some local villagers. Looking for another ten guards to train and two women to work inside. I recognize your name, so I'm assuming you are not looking for work. You brought the injured lass to Eli?"

"Aye, I came for a short visit to see how Tamsin fared and, if I may, to chat with you about your horses."

A lad came out for the horses along with another man who looked to be a villager. "We'll take care of the animals, my lord."

Thane helped Mora down, then said, "Many thanks. Our guards will brush our horses down. If you have any oats for them, we'd be appreciative."

Once the horses were taken to the stables, two females approached. Thane nodded a greeting. "Lady Grant, or should I be addressing you as Lady Grantham?" Then he turned to the other woman and said, "Greetings to you, Lady Chieftain." He wasn't quite sure how to address a female chieftain, so he hoped he was close.

Eli laughed and said, "I have not decided yet. Grant for now. That may change, though. This is Dyna, Alaric's aunt. As you already know, she and Maitland are chieftains of Clan Grantham."

"I'm pleased to meet you, Chief," he said to Maitland. "This is my sister, Mora, and my brother, Brian. We brought a few guards, but they will handle the horses. This is a neighborly visit. Mora would love to see the great hall, if you don't mind. She has some questions."

Mora's face was full of excitement, her look of awe at Dyna Grant saying it all. "You are truly a laird? A female chieftain? How did that happen? And do you like it? What is your favorite task …"

"Mora," he said, taking her hand in his. She stopped speaking, then blushed.

"Forgive me, my lady. I am excited to meet you."

"Your purpose for the visit, MacQuarie?" Maitland asked.

"I'd like to see about purchasing stud service from your warhorse, among other things. And I thought I would pass on to you that Tamsin made it to my castle just before her husband came to retrieve her. Said he was told she would be at my castle."

"And she went with him?" The look of shock on Eli's face was close to how Thane had felt the day Tamsin walked of her own volition onto her husband's ship.

"She did. She missed their daughter."

Maitland said, "Come inside for a light repast and we'll chat. I think Mora will enjoy talking with Astra, Dyna's sister, who is close to your age. She's five and ten."

"I am five and ten. I would love to meet her," Mora said, her eyes misting.

That sight alone actually sat in Thane's belly like someone had thrown a fist at him. He needed to find her friends. And he also wished to see her train in archery.

"We would enjoy visiting with you," Thane said. They moved into the great hall, surprised to see three bairns finishing up their midday meal. They greeted the wee ones, and the three picked up their miniature bows, each retrieving an arrow out just in case, he was guessing. He chuckled at the expressions on their faces.

The oldest girl approached him and said, "State your purpose." She aimed her bow directly at his belly.

Dyna, he guessed their mother, said, "Put the bows away. They are friends, Sylvi. Take your brother and sister over to play with the blocks. I need Astra for a wee bit."

Sylvi put her bow in a basket near the hearth, then ran over to the blocks and her siblings followed.

Dyna took Astra's hand and said, "This is my sister Astra. She is staying with us for a while to help. She loves to make new friends."

Mora said, "I am forever grateful to meet you, and I do hope we can be friends. Do you use a bow? I'd love to learn, if you would be willing to train me."

Dyna said, "And we would love to teach you. Come with us, and I'll find you a bow to get started with. Come along, you three," she said to her bairns. "We'll leave Eli and Maitland with the chieftain."

Mora squealed and looked at him. "May I go with them, Thane?"

"Of course. Listen well, lass," he said, pleased they were so quick to take her on. The three bairns scurried along, humming as they went.

"There is no better sound in the world than happy bairns, is there?" Eli asked, fondly watching the three depart.

Thane had no idea how to respond to her question because it was the first time he'd ever heard bairns humming. There were no bairns inside his castle. No women, no bairns. He was beginning to realize how important this was, something he could no longer ignore.

Maitland pointed to a chair by the hearth. A woman came out and Eli said, "Four ales and two meat pies, Murreal, if you please."

Once they were settled, Maitland said, "Alaric is interviewing prospective guardsmen, so he is busy. We can check with him on the way out. Before we discuss horses, please fill me in on Garvie. I need to know everyone who could be a threat to our safety. We would be in your debt if you could give us a brief review of the clans on the island—who you trust most and who not to trust."

Thane would tell them all he knew, hoping they would do a favor or two in return. "I'd be pleased to tell you what I know. Clan MacVey is the closest to you, halfway to the northernmost point where Clan Rankin sits. Both are considered allies, though their strongest alliance is to each other because of their proximity. Clan

MacQuarie sits on the western part of the isle, close to Ulva. There are MacClanes on the isle, but they are busy choosing a place to build a castle, mostly west of you. I do not speak with them much. The MacVeys have the only healer, prior to your arrival, so they see the inhabitants the most.

"Off the isle, the worst to my knowledge are the Garvies on Ulva. I know of no other clan on Ulva. Iona holds the beautiful Iona Abbey from years ago. There are some unusual features on the isle. There are two brochs, one at Dun Nan Gall and one at An Sean Chaisteal. The main mountain is Ben More in the center, and we have many caves. Our clan is the youngest as we took it over after it was ruined by fire of an unknown origin four years ago. We have restored it and have built it to a clan of five and twenty. We are always looking for more."

"What kind of a force does Garvie have?" Eli asked. "Swordsmen, archers? What do they prefer?"

"Garvie's guards carried minuscule swords when they came to retrieve Tamsin, and they were slow as a line of snails in dry dirt. It would not be difficult to take over his land if you could get your men on Ulva. I wish to visit to assess, but we only have one small ship, and I fear to lose it to Garvie's men. I don't care to be left on Ulva with no way to come across, meaning we would be at his mercy. Now that I've met him, I can tell you with complete confidence that he has no morals. He'll steal your ship and tell you he has no idea of what you speak. Do not trust him or his men."

"I don't understand why Tamsin returned to him," Eli said. "I know she wants her daughter back, and once we have the force to support her, we would go with her to assist in finding the lass."

Brian appeared stunned. "You would go into an unknown situation, put yourself and your men at risk on an island without worry?"

Eli gave a small snort. "I would if I had the right men with me. I've been in battle against the English. My archery skills are good. I believe in doing what is right, and beating a woman is wrong. He beat her because she burned his dinner, so she said."

Brian confirmed, "That is exactly what Garvie said her crime was. Said she was far from innocent. He demands a son."

"One cannot choose the gender of a bairn in your belly."

"He believes you can," Thane stated.

"Does he have archers?" Eli asked.

"I've not seen many archers on the isle. Only a few for hunting, so I doubt Garvie has any either. We have one archer, that's it."

Maitland said, "I'm going to redirect the conversation to something more useful. Tell me about the animals you hunt most. How do you feed your clan, MacQuarie?"

Thane answered, "Most on the isle depend on freshwater fishing to feed their clans, though some do sea fishing. Loch Ba, west of here a short distance, carries beautiful salmon and trout. Huge fish that will feed many. I'd be happy to take you there on another day."

"What about hunting? Boar meat the most?" Eli asked. "I love to hunt."

Brian looked surprised but said nothing, allowing his brother to answer. "We hunt red deer mostly. Especially in winter, you'll find them foraging for seaweed on the coastline. There are plenty of rodents, hares, rabbits, ferrets. We've seen some pheasant, but we've never been able to catch one. We've found some wild goats, and the clans keep many for milk. Clan Rankin had some Highland cows brought over. There has been some cattle-stealing, which had the Rankins and MacVeys in an uproar. We are still unsure who the guilty party was. They only got a couple, but they don't have a large herd yet. I'm hoping to get two of our own someday, start our own herd, but we don't have any yet."

Maitland looked at Eli and asked, "Anything else, Eli?" Then he turned to the visitors and explained, "Dyna and I are chieftains, Eli and Alaric are in charge of our guards. Swordsmen and archers."

Thane was highly impressed. A woman in charge of the guards. He'd never envisioned such a situation and hoped to see Eli in action someday. Mayhap he could hire her to train some of their guards in archery.

Eli said, "Just one question. When the hell do we go after Garvie? Seems to be the most pressing issue, Maitland."

Maitland stood and said, "Not yet, Eli. We need

to train more guards before we attack anyone. And we need to become more skilled in a ship. Then we'll talk. We need protection and food, then we consider attacking. First things first."

"Oh, spit and slime. I'll agree, Maitland, but someday I'm going after that ugly troll. Hellfire and hedgehogs."

Maitland chuckled and said, "Eli likes to curse, but trust me that she will do whatever she promises."

Thane stood and said, "Many thanks for your hospitality. Mayhap we should take our leave. If you lead me to my sister, I'll retrieve her."

Eli said, "Absolutely not. I insist that you spend the night after your journey. We have plenty of open chambers. Allow your sister to sleep in a chamber full of lasses. She'll love it. Come along. Maitland is going out to our lists, newly established and something we are excited about. You must at least agree to staying for one meal. It is the Highland way."

"I accept your hospitality and many thanks. May I follow along, Maitland?" Thane asked.

"Aye, as you wish."

Eli said, "I'll find Mora."

Thane was trying to come up with a good way to ask about paying for stud services of his warhorse when Maitland said, "We're not ready to send any horses out to use as studs yet. They need to adjust to their new home and each other first."

"When you decide you are ready, I'd be happy to bring a mare or two here."

"I'll keep that in mind. We have one more shipment of horses coming soon. Once they are all settled, I'll consider your request. Of course, our finest warhorse belongs to Alaric, so you'll have to talk with him. We have many other fine ones, but Alaric's is the best."

They arrived at the lists and Thane was stunned. He'd never seen any such thing before in his life. He let out a whistle, and Artan exited the stables. He waved him over. "Please observe with me."

He watched the men practicing their sword skills in the field in front of him, Alaric presently demonstrating by sparring with another. Thane had never seen such a demonstration of sheer physical power in his life. He had a new goal—to make himself that strong and skilled.

"Alaric's cousin Broc is sparring with him. He just arrived, and the two can spar for hours because they love it so much. They demonstrate and the new guards spend their day training."

Artan asked, "All day?"

"Most of it. We do have other work we need help with. They'll be useful in repairing some of the cottages once we can fill them. Come, I'll take you to the archery field."

They made their way to the back of the castle and their stood Mora, a bow and arrow in her hand, Dyna standing behind her, arranging her stance before she stepped back and said, "Aim and fire."

Mora shot and just missed the target. He applauded and Mora spun around, smiling. Astra shouted, "Terrific, Mora!"

Dyna approached him and said, "If you don't mind, we'd love to have Mora stay for a sennight or two. Astra would love to have a friend, and we'd be pleased to work with her in the archery field."

Mora waited expectantly until he nodded his approval. She squealed and launched herself at him, giving him a big hug.

Thane reminded her of her manners. "We'll stay the night and leave on the morrow. Aye, you may stay. You'll help wherever you can, Mora. They need help getting the castle established."

"Of course! But I brought only enough clothing for one night."

Dyna said, "Astra has more than she needs, and you are close in size. Plus, I insist on fitting you with your first pair of leggings and matching tunic, the only clothing a female archer should wear."

Mora giggled with more excitement than he'd ever seen. Thane had a sudden odd thought as he watched Dyna with his sister.

Had he been wrong all these years about women?

CHAPTER NINETEEN

Thane

*Eight years ago, late spring,
unknown island*

THANE RIPPED OUT another weed, then used the shovel to dig a hole in the ground before sticking the roots of the small plant into it. He covered it with soil, so the leaves were visible out of the top. His belly growled at just the thought that this plant would someday be edible.

He'd had naught but a few beans to break his fast before his mother had sent him out to the garden with his brother. "Get out there before it gets too hot. The plants wither if you plant them at high sun. Brian, you water after Thane plants. And get all those weeds out or there'll be one lash for every weed you miss."

Brian shivered as he tugged out another weed and put it in the bucket nearby. "Help me, Thane. Do not let me miss any." His brother whispered almost everything he ever said.

"I'll watch, Brian." He glanced over his shoulder

to make sure she'd gone inside. "I'll check when we're finished to make sure we've not missed anything."

He wouldn't allow her to hit him ever again. She'd used the whip on them once and Thane swore it would never happen again.

"Do you think Da will ever return?" Brian whispered.

Thane said, "Nay. We've never met him, so he's either dead or doesn't want us. I think the latter."

The door opened and his mother tossed Mora outside, the tears covering her face. "Get out there. All you do is cry. Shut your mouth. I tire of listening to you."

"Mama, I'm hungry."

"Blame your brothers. They ate all I had." Then the door shut, and Mora ran over to Thane's side.

Thane took a break long enough to wrap his arm around his sister, but then the door opened, and their mother shouted, "Get back to work, Thane." She held a wooden board in her hand and slapped it against her thigh for effect.

Brian jumped and Mora clung to Thane, burying her face in his shoulder. He set her off to the side and whispered, "Just for a few moments. She'll be napping soon. Let me put two more in the ground, then I've got a piece of oatcake for you."

Mora wiped her tears and sat in the dirt, watching her brothers work, kneading her filthy gown in her hands.

Every night, Thane spent half the night trying to figure out how he could get them away from their mother and her cruelty. At ten winters old, he was old enough to work and take care of his siblings.

Someday soon, he'd find a way to get away from here, and he'd never return.

One of the things he hated most was how their mother always silenced Mora whenever she spoke. Sometimes it was a slap, other times it was water thrown in her face. When she was truly miserable, she would hang Mora on a peg on the wall, throwing something at her whenever she talked.

Mora learned how to be silent. Most of the time.

He vowed he would get the two siblings and himself away. Once, he'd had a plan to run away, after which he would return for them, but he had to cancel that plan because he'd never be able to stand being away from his brother and sister. He would be too worried about how they suffered in his absence.

He couldn't do it to Brian or Mora.

If they could just get away.

But he had never imagined their life could be any worse until the day it was. Their mother woke up one morning about a year later and discovered that Brian had found her hidden supply of oatcakes and eaten two in the middle of the night.

Hopping mad, she grabbed a sack, threw a few clothes inside, and said, "That's it. I've had enough of you whiny piglets. You're moving out."

Mora wailed, and Brian couldn't stop babbling,

but they were ushered down to a dock they'd never seen, forced into a boat, the sack thrown in with them, and then another man came along and started rowing.

Mora cried all the while they were in the boat, climbing onto Thane's lap and gripping him so tight whenever the boat rocked that she drew blood from his arm. They flew across the sea until they could see nothing but water all around them. Before long, the boat landed on a beach. His mother got out, grabbed Brian by the hair, and dragged him onto the shore.

"Get out, Thane, and bring that whiny lass with you."

"What are we supposed to do, Mama? When will you return for us?" Brian asked, though he stood far enough away to avoid her fists.

She grabbed the sack, tossed it onto the beach, and said, "Never. You are on your own. I never wish to see any of you ever again."

The man rowing spun around to stare at her. At the last minute, he grabbed a pouch from the seat next to him and tossed it at them.

And the boat left.

The man's last words were, "Don't stay in the sun too long. It will burn your skin."

Thane watched the two leave, such hatred leaking from every pore in his body that it was lucky he was young, or he would have swum out after them to tip the boat over. He wished to scream and cry and carry on, but the longer he stood there, the happier he was.

Brian looked at his brother and asked, "Why aren't you upset that they left us here alone?"

Thane smiled and replied, "Because it's what I always dreamed would happen. That I would steal away from the bitch and take you both with me." He shrugged his shoulders. "We'll be fine without her. We don't need her."

Mora and Brian stared at him, their faces frozen with fear—glassy eyes, sweat on their foreheads, quivering lips. He took one hand of each and said, "Don't you see? We're free. We can do what we want, and we'll never be slapped again. No whips, no paddles, no pegs. And we can talk as loud and as much as we wish to."

Brian's face crumpled. "But what will we do?"

"Whatever we like. First, we'll walk until we can find a place to sleep. Not on the beach. Mayhap we could find a cave. You know the one we were in long ago? With Da?"

Brian and Mora both shook their heads.

"You don't remember."

Two heads shook again.

"Then come along. We'll find a cave. But first, I wish to see what we have." He opened the sack his mother had packed and found a second outfit and mantle for each of them. There was a hat for Mora, some hair ties, a comb, a few oatcakes, and a chunk of soap. Some woolen hose for winter. That was it.

He wasn't surprised. Brian brought him the rower's pouch and said, "What do you suppose he left us?"

Thane took a deep breath and untied it, peeking inside, then letting out a huge sigh.

"What is it?" Brian asked.

"Quite a bit of dried meat, and something even more valuable."

"What?" Mora asked. "Can we see, Thane?"

He held up a dagger, something they would need to survive.

"Good. I'm glad we have meat. But why do we need a knife? And how does that help us at all? Why did he leave it?"

Brian said, "Stop asking so many questions, Mora."

"Nay, Brian. From now on, Mora can ask as many questions as she wants."

Thus began Mora's penchant for asking multiple questions at once.

He looked up at the sun and said, "We have half a day to find a cave as it could be cold and wet tonight."

That was the beginning of their adventure. They'd found a cave and learned to live on their own. They lived off berries, greens, apples, and anything they could forage. Waterfalls became their favorite place because they could wash and have fun at the same time. They became very skinny, but they were happy.

Every once in a while, they'd awaken and find a pouch of dried meat left just inside the cave. They treasured that meat, but no matter how they tried, they never discovered who left it.

They met a few more along the way and their

group grew until three years later when they found the deserted castle and one more important piece.

Artan.

He taught them how to start a fire and skin meat and catch fish.

Brian and Mora never looked back.

Thane did. He lived for vengeance, and someday, he'd find her.

CHAPTER TWENTY

Tamsin

WHEN HE FINISHED, Raghnall headed to the door and stopped while Tamsin set her gown to rights. This was her husband. It was the act every married couple performed, yet every incident left her ashamed and even a bit disgusted.

"I'll say this about you, wife. Even after a bairn, you still have sweet curves. Because of that, I'll allow you to see our daughter on this day for the midday meal. I will have Extilda bring Alana to you at supper time. Until that time, you are to remain in this chamber. And a fair warning to you—you will not repeat to anyone what transpired between the time I left you in the sea and now. If you do, your visits with our daughter will end forever. Understood?"

"Aye, my lord."

Raghnall was no lord, but he insisted on being called as such.

She climbed off the oversized bed and went

to the basin of water to clean herself. Relations always made her feel unclean, even dirty, but that was mostly because her husband did not believe in washing more than once a fortnight.

When she finished, Tamsin moved over to one of the two chairs in front of the hearth, then sat down and picked up the garment she'd started for her dear daughter. Tears misted her gaze as she looked at the bodice she'd created. How she adored the lass. Alana's hair was a shade brighter red than her own, and both eyes were green, unlike Tamsin's differently colored eyes.

She let out a light squeal of excitement when the door burst open, and her sweet lass ran across the chamber and jumped into her arms with a giggle. "Mama!" At less than two years, her speaking mostly consisted of one or two-word expressions, but they were clear and loud.

Extilda followed her inside the chamber, setting a tray of food on the small table next to her. "Many thanks to you, Extilda."

The woman gave her a look of pity, something she wasn't used to. Extilda wasn't known for her kindness, and she rarely spoke, so what happened next totally surprised Tamsin.

"Your supper, my lady. And I'm sorry to hear of your troubles. You do not deserve such horrific treatment."

Tamsin patted her maid's hand but said nothing, Raghnall's words fresh in her mind.

Extilda turned around and took her leave, saying nothing more. Tamsin froze, watchful as the woman left. What exactly had been said

about her? Raghnall seemed to believe that no
one knew anything about her experience.

But servants loved to gossip. Either way, she
let the thoughts fade so she could give her full
attention to her daughter.

"Alana, Mama missed you so much," she
declared, fighting the tears. Her daughter was
more adorable than ever. She had the greenest
eyes, and her hair had soft waves that often had a
mind of their own.

"Miss you," Alana said, cupping both her
mother's cheeks in her hands, a movement that
nearly made her cry, but she forced a broad smile
instead.

"You are even lovelier than the last time I saw
you, my sweet girl."

"Berries, pweez?" Her lashes had grown even
longer in her absence.

"Aye, have some berries. And some bread too."

Her daughter's eyes danced with pleasure, the
sparkle of happiness there, something she'd fought
to bear witness to every day of her daughter's life.

Sometimes it was a battle.

"Where have you been, Alana?" While she
feared her husband might be eavesdropping, she
had to find out the truth of what had happened
to her little girl. Raghnall hadn't forbidden her
from asking Alana any questions.

"Gramama's." She took a bite of a berry and
the juice squirted out of her mouth and down
her chin, bringing an infectious giggle to the
surface as she watched her mother.

Tamsin's heart ached with the love inside her

for this child, but also ached for the child she'd lost. Had the bairn been a wee laddie or a lassie? She had loved the time she'd been able to nurse Alana, holding her close, inhaling her scent. She'd spent hours just running her fingers across the babe's soft skin. The fact that she carried a child inside her and not known it saddened her more than she cared to admit.

But so much saddened her that the pain had been engulfed by other events. Fighting for her life and watching all that transpired at Clan Grantham had nearly made her forget she lost the bairn. The wondrous part of her life had been sneaking out to peek at Thane MacQuarie's acts designed to protect her from Raghnall. His efforts had warmed her heart more than she would have ever guessed.

Raghnall was as mad as the banshee in the dark forest at night at Thane and she liked it. She couldn't help but wonder what it would feel like to be married to someone like Thane. Alas, that was not to be her station in life. She wiped her daughter's chin with the linen square on the tray.

Alana's nose wrinkled and she leaned toward her mother. "No yike Gramama."

"You must treat her kindly, love," Tamsin said, her mind rushing to find another explanation to convince Alana to be nice. Angering Dagga would not be in the child's best interest.

The woman was so evil, she would indeed take that anger out on a wee bairn.

"Did she hurt you, sweeting?"

"Mean," she said with a mouthful of bread.

"Chew your food first, lass." Every move Alana made put a smile on Tamsin's face. She took the time to say a quick prayer for her, using the sign of the cross on her to keep the evil forces at bay.

If only she could find out where Alana's grandmother was.

Extilda had been kind enough that her next move might be to ask her.

She'd risk anything for Alana. Anything.

The door banged open and there, filling the doorway, stood Raghnall, the fury on his face worse than she'd ever seen it.

Alana let out a wee squeal, then smiled at her father. Tamsin pulled her daughter in close to protect her.

He could beat Tamsin as much as he wanted, but not Alana.

CHAPTER TWENTY-ONE

Thane

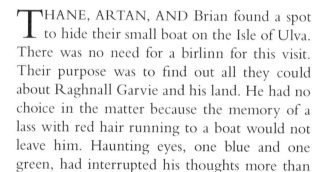

THANE, ARTAN, AND Brian found a spot to hide their small boat on the Isle of Ulva. There was no need for a birlinn for this visit. Their purpose was to find out all they could about Raghnall Garvie and his land. He had no choice in the matter because the memory of a lass with red hair running to a boat would not leave him. Haunting eyes, one blue and one green, had interrupted his thoughts more than he would care to admit.

Watching Tamsin run down to her husband's boat had struck him, piercing his heart in a way he hadn't expected. He was anxious to see what they would find out about Garvie, though he wasn't ready to admit the reason why it meant so much to him.

If he did, it would be admitting he had feelings for a lass, something he swore would never happen before Tamsin came into his life.

They'd studied the coastline and decided to travel on the north end a bit, always observant of the cliffs in the south. Not wanting to leave their boat near the shortest distance from Mull to Ulva, they decided to go around the tip to the south in search of a spot where they could hide their boat and where the foot traffic was much less.

They needed the boat to return home.

Artan pointed to a spot where the coastline was flat with a few places to hide the small vessel, so they ventured there, pleased to see no one was about.

"I wish we had horses."

Artan said, "I was told Garvie's holdings are not far from this spot. There are few other inhabitants on the isle. Take over Garvie's land, and the isle could be yours."

Thane listened, but his mind was intent on taking in all he needed to learn about the isle—the landscape, wildlife, boats, any inhabitants, and buildings. It was beautiful, lush with greenery and birdlife, including Mora's favorite, the puffins, that were abundant on the coastline.

Her squeal whenever she caught sight of a group of puffins was a treat for him. He missed her already, having left her at the Grantham holding to spend time with Astra while she was visiting.

He knew she needed female companionship, and he could think of none better than Eli, Dyna, and Astra. Mora hoped to learn some archery, and she would benefit from her time around the bairns, another pastime she had little experience with.

No women living on their land meant no bairns

living with them. Wee ones visited occasionally with their fathers—guards, carpenters, armorers. But Mora rarely had the chance to experience bairns.

Thane looked forward to listening to her chatter about all her new experiences.

For now, his focus was on taking out the evil of the world—Raghnall Garvie. The world would be better off without him.

They made their way to a small village consisting of several merchants hawking their wares. The three headed down the middle of town, observing men at the armorer, the fish market, the baker, and others.

Thane purchased a loaf of bread and split it between the three of them, then began asking questions. "How often is the market open?"

"I only come across the loch one day every sennight. I don't like it here of late."

Thane arched a brow and said nothing, knowing that the man would expand on his comments if he didn't respond.

The merchant glanced around as if he were waiting to be struck down for speaking his mind, then leaned forward. "The man who controls the isle gets meaner every day."

Thane handed his brother and Artan each another hunk of bread, then motioned for them to keep watch for anyone who would interrupt them. He knew Artan would keep others away until he got the information he sought. "Who controls all?"

"Garvie," the merchant whispered, so low

Thane strained to hear him. "He's such an evil man that he nearly killed his own wife, and she's a beauty. The man is daft."

Thane took a bite of his bread and said, "Fine bread you make. Please tell me more."

"Many thanks to you. They say he beats her nearly every day. I heard he wants her dead, so he can marry another to give him a son. Said he's trying to get every unmarried lass around carrying and whichever one gets a big belly the fastest will be his new wife."

"His wife never gave him a bairn?"

The man snorted. "Aye, a pretty lass, but she stays with his mother. She keeps her locked up because she hates bairns. In fact, I heard an awful fact, and I fear to even repeat it. But if it's true, others need to know what takes place on the island."

Thane leaned forward but said nothing, while Brian and Artan continued to scan the area for trouble.

"They say the bitch sells bairns. Takes them to other islands and sells them. Puts them on ships for coin. They must be older than two winters. That's how the fools make their coin. There are several cottages on his land where the ones who work for him stay. Guards, cooks, carpenters, those kind. I wish to leave and never return, but he comes after me on Mull."

Thane stood back, the hairs on his neck bristling with a sudden understanding of more than he wished. "Where is Garvie's holding?"

The man pointed to the west. "Follow that

path. Though you'll not get past his guards. The only way to any other part on the isle is to land on the coast to the west."

"So where are the other holdings on the isle? Any castles? Brochs?"

"Nay. Just Garvie. He's taken them all over as his own. Anyone who built or lived in a hut has been sent away. We are the only ones allowed because he needs our wares. And if we don't come, he comes after us."

There was only one thing more that Thane needed to know before he made his decision about what to do with Garvie.

"How many men?"

The man shrugged his shoulders. "I'd guess three score. No more."

That was all the information he needed. With his own men and the guards of Clan Grantham, he might be able to accomplish his goal. But it would take time. He didn't have the men to attack yet, and he had no idea if Clan Grantham did either.

Thane paid the man for another loaf of bread and sauntered back to Brian and Artan, filling them in on all he'd learned.

"I say we return," Brian said. "No reason to head to Garvie land."

Artan said, "I agree. We are not prepared to fight anyone."

"I've learned enough for this day." Thane led the way back toward the place where they'd hidden the boat. They glanced around before heading in that direction, making sure they were not being followed, but none had expected to find what they did.

A lad of mayhap ten summers sat inside their boat, his arms crossed in front of him.

The three men stopped to stare at the lad, but he was not frozen, instead speaking his mind quickly, his words coming out in such a rush that Thane almost didn't hear everything.

"Take me with you. Anywhere away from the island. I know why you are here because I followed you, but I need your help. My sister and I were sent here to be sold. We escaped a sennight ago, but we wish to be away from the isle. If you take us with you, I'll tell you all you need to know about the Garvie holding."

Artan responded faster than Thane even thought possible. "Where is your sister?"

The lad pointed to a spot around the corner toward the coastline. The three men stepped around some trees, and there sat a blond-haired lass of around five, her hands folded demurely in her lap.

Thane held his hand out to her, and she got up and took it. "I shall go with Magni, wherever that may be, if you please."

"Is Magni your brother?" Thane led her back around to the boat where the lad was, now standing next to it. He knew what it felt like to be left alone on an island you'd never been to before. He surely would not leave these two behind.

"Aye."

"What's your name?" Thane asked, wondering what the hell kind of game Garvie was playing.

"Lia. Will you be our new papa?"

Thane didn't know exactly how to answer that, but he did his best to be honest, so he knelt in front of her and waved her brother over. "I'll take you both back to our castle. We will not sell you, but you may choose to stay with us, or I can try to find parents to take you in. We'll feed you, though Magni may have some chores to do, and we'll give you a pallet inside, so you'll be warm, but I promise to keep you away from Garvie. That is all I can offer you. Do you accept, Magni? I ask you to speak for both of you."

Magni nodded, tears coming to his eyes, but he brushed them away. "Aye, we will come with you. I promise to work verra hard, and I wish to take any beatings for my sister. She is too young."

"There will be no beatings, Magni, for you or your sister." Others believed in beating bairns, but Thane did not. After witnessing the look of relief on both of their faces, he smiled, then said, "Climb in."

Magni and Lia hugged him first.

What the hell was he going to do with two orphans?

He certainly would not leave them alone like his mother had done to him.

CHAPTER TWENTY-TWO

Tamsin

TAMSIN SURELY HAD a curse on her head. This time, she never said a word when her husband dropped her on a rock in the middle of the sea. She shivered after the boat disappeared in the mist, but didn't bother yelling after Raghnall. He was leaving her to die. Again. Of that much she was certain. She would not give him the satisfaction of begging.

He hadn't taken her as far out this time. He didn't need to. With a broken or sprained ankle, there was little she could do. The injury she'd had before had only worsened when he forced her down to the dock, dragging her across the uneven terrain.

He left her when the tide was low, but she had no idea how much time she had until the water would rise. She scanned the area, only to see that the rocky coastline appeared to go on forever. This area was completely different from the previous place she'd been left. If she knew her husband, he made sure it was more secluded than before so she would not be rescued. She sat up as tall as she could, shivering as a cool breeze swept across her skin.

To one side, all she saw was water, the sea waves rougher than she liked, mostly due to the wind, if she were to guess. But what the hell did she know of the sea, the tides, and weather?

She'd better learn quickly if she ever wished to see her daughter again.

To the other side, she could see land clearly, but it was a distance away. Not long if she were her usual self and could swim or walk, but neither of those were available to her now.

She couldn't swim, and with an injured leg, she was nearly helpless. Or so the bastard thought.

She vowed to prove him wrong, and only for her dearest Alana.

When Tamsin glanced across the multitude of rocks that could be seen above water, she knew there was a chance. She would have to move from one rock to the next because, in a few hours, all these rocks would be underwater, invisible to anyone looking out to the sea.

It was her only chance. She couldn't count on Thane MacQuarie to save her on this day.

Her leg was useless, so she would be forced to crawl, but she believed it was possible. Taking a deep breath, she arranged herself on all fours, pleased that her chin was above water level enough to move along and not drown.

Not yet, anyway. It was going to be a battle, moving quickly enough to stay ahead of the incoming tide.

"Ow," she cried out, not caring how loud she was, her voice echoing in the early-morning air. *Do not look, do not look, do not look.* She forced herself not to glance down, knowing that the rough surface of the rock had sliced the tender skin on her knee. Blood was something she'd prefer not to look at, and stopping would slow her progress.

Closing her eyes, she thought of her daughter, humming her favorite song, recalling the sweet lilt of her wee one's voice as she tried to sing along with Tamsin. Any person who was that loveable and innocent did not deserve Raghnall for a father or his mother as her grandmother.

Tamsin had lost her mother when she was ten summers. Her memories were still strong, so she sang the same tunes her mother had sung for her and her sister. Their father had struggled to raise them, confused as to how to handle two lasses, thus he had spent as much time away from them as he could manage. They were alone from dawn to dusk, doing their best to do what their mother had done: cleaning, planting, washing, cooking. But it never suited their sire because they were not fast enough or good enough, his bellowing often bringing tears to her sister. Poor Meg.

Tamsin had learned to be strong early in life. It would serve her well now.

Moving on to the next rock, she winced when a spot on her palm caught on a sharp edge, ripping her tender skin.

She didn't care. Pain would not stop her. Continuing ahead, she proceeded to the following rock, crawling slowly because of her wounds, but the next rock was not flat as the others had been. She slipped into a crevice and had to stand on her one leg to get her face back above water. Flailing when she slipped again, she did what she could to keep her head up.

Surprised that the flailing had moved her up instead of down, she tried it again, moving her arms in a wild pattern of constant movement, pleased to find it helped her. Was this how one swam?

She vowed to learn how to swim if she made it out of this predicament.

Keeping her eye on the sun to track the time, she continued in the same way. She moved forward, cut another part of her knee, a part of her other hand, closed her eyes and imagined Alana standing on land calling to her, and plugged along.

Tamsin crawled, cut herself, fell into crevices, flailed, cried a bit, cut the top of her foot, drank salty water, spit, and cried a little more.

But she never stopped. The sun moved to its highest spot, turning her skin a shade of red, if she were to guess, before she was nearly at the coastline. Grass was not far away, just on the other side of the small stretch of sand, but she knew the grass was the only place she would be safe from the rising tide. Sometimes it covered all the sand, depending on the location.

This spot was unfamiliar, so she had to be careful.

She vowed to make it to the grass because it

was the safest place. At least if she were to die there, someone would find her. If Raghnall had his way, she would wash out to sea, never to be found again.

Alana would never know what happened to her mother. She was sure her evil mother-in-law would tell the girl that her mother had deserted her.

As she moved along, fatigue plagued her. Raghnall had hauled her out of their bed late at night, so she had little sleep, the worries always there in her mind.

She started, shook her head, and shivered. The water was up to her chin, waking her from a brief nap, something she hadn't known she'd done. *I cannot sleep, cannot sleep, cannot …*

Her eyelids fluttered closed again, but she forced them open. She knew that in order to survive, she had to get to land. It was the only way.

But if I took a wee nap here, I could make it to the grass. Then I would be safe. If I don't, I'll never make it. A wee nap, just for a moment. Then I'll be safe forever.

Just for a few moments, then I'll continue …

CHAPTER TWENTY-THREE

Thane

MAGNI PROVED TO be quite inquisitive. Thane had to smile at the lad's continuous onslaught of questions, only to be stunned by the amazing insight wee Lia offered about her brother and their situation, her golden hair coming free of its plait as the group rode their horses back to the castle. Lia sat in front of Thane while Magni rode with Artan, firing questions about everything he saw.

Lia patted Thane's hand and whispered, "May I speak freely?"

"Please do. Talk as you wish, lassie." Thane couldn't help but grin at her maturity for her age. Mora would love this girl.

"You are probably wondering why he talks so. We were not allowed to speak because we are bairns."

"By Garvie?"

"Mostly his mother. Bairns are ignorant, stupid, and…idjits. I think those were her words. He will be happy if he is free to ask his questions."

"You both may speak whenever you wish, as long as you do not keep us awake at night."

"Magni has a verra quick mind."

"And where are your parents?"

"Our village was attacked on Coll. They killed all the elders and took the children to various isles. We ended up on Ulva."

Thane couldn't believe how well-spoken the child was.

"I'm nearly six."

Could she read his mind too?

They approached the gates, and Magni finally stopped speaking, the awe that crossed his face at the sight of the castle something to watch.

"Is this our new home?" Lia asked.

"If you wish it to be," Thane answered. "You may take your time to think on it." Why he said such a thing, he didn't know. Ever since he'd seen Tamsin tossed on a rock, everything he believed had been challenged. He didn't trust females, other than Mora, but now he'd met Dyna and Eli, two skilled and honest women.

He said he would never have bairns about because they were too much work.

And now he had a lass of nearly six in front of him, and she and her brother had made him smile more times since he'd met them than he'd smiled in the last year.

"Lia, look at our new home!" Magni's arms pointed over his head, his excitement contagious.

They crossed the bridge, were let in the gates, then headed to the stables. As soon as Magni's feet hit the ground, he took off at a sprint, tearing in circles as he examined his surroundings.

In the time it took for Thane to dismount, lower Lia to the ground, and hand the reins to Theo, Magni had already run through the stables, across the courtyard, up the steps to the keep and back again.

Bearnard stopped in front of Thane, looked down, and said, "A lass? Where'd you get her, Chief?"

"Found them on Ulva. No parents and they were mistreated by their previous owner. This is Lia and her brother Magni. They are staying with us for now."

Lia smiled and said, "Greetings to you, dear sir. My, but you are both quite tall. Would you be so kind as to pick me up, my lord Thane?"

Thane didn't know what to say because he hadn't held any young ones since Mora was small. His guard sensed it, apparently, because Bearnard stepped up quickly. He held both hands out to Lia. "What about me? I'm nearly as tall as he is. Come see from up here?"

Lia reached for Bearnard with a smile, and the guard's reaction was swift. He swung the girl up in the air until she landed on his shoulders with a squeal, grabbing his head with both hands to steady herself.

"Now, you cannot cover my eyes, lassie, but I'll give you a ride into the keep, if you like." Then he winked at Thane and said, "My daughter loves it, Chief."

"Lia?" Thane glanced at her to see her reaction,

feeling he should ask her, but from her giggles, he surmised she was fine with it.

"Aye, please," she said.

"Be careful," Thane said, immediately thinking he was turning daft.

Once inside the great hall, Bearnard set Lia in a chair near the hearth, then threw more wood onto the embers, stoking it. Magni rushed over and hugged his sister. "We'll like it here, Lia. I'm sure of it."

Agnes came out of the kitchens, stopping in her tracks. "Bairns, my lord?"

"Aye, mistreated ones with no parents. Do we have any porridge and honey left? And if you could ready them a chamber for this eve together, I'd appreciate it."

"I'll have some porridge in a few minutes." Agnes disappeared.

"Magni, I'll take you outside and you can tell me all you know about the isle. Brian will stay with you, Lia."

Brian had come in behind him. "I'd be pleased to sit with the lass."

Thane led Magni outside, headed to the guardhouse, then said to him, "Tell me about Garvie and his wife."

"The one he is trying to kill? Tamsin?"

The lad looked up at him with such innocence, Thane couldn't believe it. "Does everyone know he's trying to kill his own wife?"

"Aye, everyone but Tamsin and their daughter Alana."

Thane cursed. The man was sheer evil. "Has he tried before?"

"Once, but now he is set to try again. I heard him say he would take her out some night soon and leave her."

Thane absorbed what Magni said and strode across to the back gate, leading Magni outside. "Follow me. This is my favorite place. I can see all the sea from here. It is quite a peaceful spot."

He came to a halt at his favorite location. From this vantage point, he could see how many ships were at sea, how high the tide was, and any approaching visitors from the path behind the castle. Not many used it, preferring to travel along the coast, but his clan used it frequently. It was the best path to take into the forest for hunting.

"This is amazing. I can see forever," Magni said, truly enthralled by the view, but Thane didn't tarry.

They continued on for a short distance, following the well-worn path, Thane's mind filled with questions about their future. So much had changed recently.

"Look," Magni cried. "Is that not something odd on the coastline? Is that a body?"

Thane's gaze went to the same place immediately, shocked he hadn't noticed it himself. But he was also grateful to the lad. If he were to wager, the body was Tamsin Garvie.

Thane took off toward the coast, Magni behind him, but he shouted, "Magni, go to the stables and tell Theo to ready five horses. Meet me down there with two of them."

"Aye, Chief. I'll take care of everything." Magni took off, humming as he went. Was the lad happy all the time or was it a reflection of his new home?

Thane had more important things to focus on. A body.

CHAPTER TWENTY-FOUR

Thane

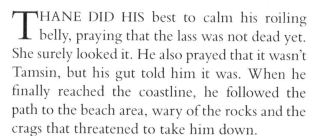

THANE DID HIS best to calm his roiling belly, praying that the lass was not dead yet. She surely looked it. He also prayed that it wasn't Tamsin, but his gut told him it was. When he finally reached the coastline, he followed the path to the beach area, wary of the rocks and the crags that threatened to take him down.

The smell of the salty water caught him as it always did, and he breathed it in deeply, something he did to remind himself that he was free, that there was no spiteful mother hiding anywhere to slap him or beat his brother while he watched.

All the memories of past injustices surfaced as he raced toward the body, the hair becoming darker red the closer he came to it. The person's face was hidden beneath a blanket of hair, the strands interlaced with the green kelp of the sea.

He knelt next to the body, quite sure it was Tamsin, but he had to see her face to know for sure. Then the most wonderful thing happened— she moved. Covered in sand and sea and kelp, he gingerly pushed her hair back. "Tamsin? It's me, Thane."

Nothing.

He placed his fingers on the side of her neck where the blood beat the strongest, pleased to find an even pulse against his skin. She lay on her side, so he rolled her back into the grass, and her eyes fluttered open but quickly shut again.

"Tamsin?" He cupped her cheek, his thumb brushing the sand crystals away, doing his best to straighten her loose strands of hair.

Magni came flying down the hill toward him, one horse behind him. "The other horses are getting prepared for you, Chief. Artan will bring them along. Is she dead? Is it Lady Garvie?"

Thane lifted his gaze to the lad, surprised at how quickly he'd accomplished his task. "She's not dead, and aye, it is Lady Garvie."

Magni brought the horse as close as he could to him, and he was glad of it because there was no time to waste, or the lass would surely die. He had no desire to watch her pass in his arms.

"Hold the horse still. I'll lay her across and then climb up."

He lifted the lass, and she stirred, her hands clutching at his chest just before her eyes opened, falling on him, the fear inside so clear it was like a fist punch to his belly. When she recognized him, the look in her gaze changed instantly to one of hope, not what he expected.

There was something about the way she looked at him that warmed his heart. Did he even have a heart to be warmed? Sometimes he wondered if it had been ripped and stomped on by his mother so much that it had become minuscule and incapable of emotion.

Tamsin Garvie made him think otherwise.

"Magni, get on the other side so you can keep her from falling off while I mount. You'll have to follow us back up the path."

"I can do both."

He held Tamsin close while Magni arranged the horse. Then he did the oddest thing.

He kissed her cheek. "Tamsin?"

Thane held her close, looking at her flawless skin, the lips that should be pink and rosy instead of tinged with gray. Willing her eyes to open, he shifted her weight toward the animal to block the breeze, warming her up as much as he could.

But she didn't awaken.

He settled her on the horse, the beast only moving a bit until he patted its flank, then climbed up behind her.

When Thane sat her up to lean back against him for his heat, he caught a change in Magni's expression. The boy stared up at him and smiled. "She's awake, Chief."

"Tamsin?"

Her gaze settled on Magni and the words that came out unsettled him. "Alana? You are hale? Papa did not punish you?"

Magni said, "I'm not Alana, but I know where she is."

Tamsin gasped before her eyes closed again.

"Magni, we're going to take her inside and have Agnes change her into dry clothing. Then we're heading to Duart Castle. Are you ready for a journey?"

"Aye, Chief. And Lia too."

"And Magni? Great eyes. I don't know if I would have noticed her. You've saved a life today, lad. I'm proud of you. We'll meet you in the keep."

"Aye, Chief." The lad beamed, his brown hair wild from the sea breeze, but his smile lit up his face. Thane was pleased to have found the two cherubs, but now he had to focus on Tamsin.

He had to get her to Eli Grant at Clan Grantham.

CHAPTER TWENTY-FIVE

Eli

ELI RUBBED HER hands together in front of the hearth. Hellfire, but it had all seemed too real.

Dyna came up behind her, handing her a goblet of wine. "This bottle is from the ones Maitland found in the cellar the first day. It is fine wine, and the wee ones are in bed, so it is time to enjoy it. You are done hunting, right?"

"Aye," she said, taking the goblet a wee bit too anxiously. She took two huge gulps of the fragrant liquid. It tasted better than it smelled, of that she was certain.

Dyna arched a brow and took a seat in front of the hearth. "You must still think it was Logan."

"I do! I cannot get it out of my mind. How I wish you had been there, Dyna. Alaric wasn't looking in the right place. He never saw him, and I'm not sure he would have recognized him if he had seen him." She set her goblet on a nearby table and fell into the chair with a flop.

"It is difficult to be certain of someone's identity if you only see their back."

"But I know Grandsire. I know his walk, the way he sits his horse. It was him."

"It surely is possible. Logan has been known to show up at the oddest places at the strangest times. Grandsire said they called him the wanderer when he was young because he would take off and not tell anyone. They never knew where he was or when he would return. But I think he always has his reasons for his adventures, so that brings up the question—why do you think he would be here?" Dyna asked, taking another sip of her wine before she sat down, crossing her legs.

"I don't know." Eli's grandparents had disappeared in late spring after she had married Alaric. Her grandmother was having a terrible time with her knee, unable to stop the pus from draining and causing intense pain. After visiting and being treated by various healers, she'd given up and said she was leaving, going to die in peace with Grandsire. She wished to die privately.

That was the last time Eli had seen them. Grandsire had said he would be back, so it was possible he could be here on the isle. Her grandmother was probably dead, though it pained her much to think on it. "You know I named my mare Golden Gwyn."

"Aye, it's a fine name. No reason to change it. Mayhap you should name your horse Gwynie. That would bring your grandfather back, would it not?"

Dyna's slanted grin told Eli she knew the tale

as much as she did. Her grandsire, Logan Ramsay, had always called his wife Gwynie. But he would not allow anyone else to use that name. "So true, Dyna. Cadyn tried to call her that once, and Grandsire nearly threw him across the hall."

Warm thoughts brought her back to her beloved grandmother. She surely had passed on. Aunt Brenna and Aunt Jennie had both said there was naught more they could do for her. But what about her grandfather? Where had he gone? Would he return to Ramsay land?

"It makes no sense. There is absolutely no reason for him to be here, and if he were, he would visit."

Maitland came along and said, "I couldn't help but overhear your conversation. I agree. Logan would visit. I don't envision him hiding out from any of us. If he were on Mull, he would be here. I think your mind is telling you what you wish the truth was."

Eli sighed, refusing to let a tear loose. They were right, she knew it, but it still hurt. "I know you speak the truth. I'm always hopeful. I've wished and prayed for them both to return, but it is not to be."

The door opened and Alaric shouted, "Eli, Tamsin is back."

"Oh, my goodness. How bad?" Eli asked, bolting out of her chair and nearly spilling her wine.

"It looks bad. Ready the chamber, and I'll help MacQuarie get her in here."

Eli hurried into her chamber after telling

Murreal all she would need. Hot water, goat's milk if they had any, along with many linen squares. And she hoped Tamsin could take some broth.

Dyna said, "I'll go with you. My guess is that this won't be pretty because this is his second attack. Thane saved her before, so I'm guessing the bully made certain she wouldn't survive this time."

"Then Thane's saved her again? Or did he set him up?" Eli couldn't imagine having to deal with all poor Tamsin had to deal with. She would surely stick a blade in her husband's heart when he was sleeping, or mayhap somewhere else. Her grin at the thought caught Dyna.

Dyna laughed. "I know what you are thinking, and I would do the same. Right in his private parts."

The two giggled about that thought until they both stopped. Dyna chewed on her lip and crossed her arms. "Do you suppose Garvie might attack Thane's castle while he's gone? Could that be possible?"

Eli let out a low whistle. "Let's hope not. Poor Thane." She couldn't help but think about how he'd become involved in a marital affair between two strangers, yet he'd acted as honorably as any Highlander. "Your grandsire would have been proud of Thane, Dyna."

The door opened and Alaric held it open for Thane to enter.

"Set her here, Thane. Is she awake?"

He shook his head. "She awakened once when

Magni spoke to her, but we think she thought Magni was her daughter."

"Magni?" Eli looked behind the men but saw no one.

Then a lad jumped inside the door. "Me! I'm here. May I please bring my sister Lia in to sit? She's tired."

Eli chuckled as the cutest lad she'd seen in a long time—wavy dark hair to his shoulders with one plait at the front—jumped inside, a golden-haired lass half his size following behind him. She beamed with a smile.

"May I sit inside where it is safe, if you please? I pledge not to be a bother." Dressed in a dirty gown with worn boots that were too big for her, Eli glanced at Dyna, who reacted faster than she ever could.

"Come right over here, Lia. Magni, you stay with Thane. Lia, sit over here by the fire, take off those ill-fitting boots, and warm yourself. Here's a fur to warm your feet and I'll find you a clean gown. But not until I find a warm tub for you once the men depart."

Lia smiled and gave a small bow as if she were the queen of the land, her natural sparkle lighting up the chamber. "Many thanks to you for your kindness. And while I bathe, you can all tell me what your wishes are."

Dyna's head turned toward the lass. "Wishes? We don't have any special wishes."

"Well, I only have one. I wish my grandmother was still alive."

"You miss her?" Lia asked.

"Aye. More than you would understand. I adore her and she left too soon. I would love it if my grandparents were both on the isle. But she has passed on, I'm sure."

Dyna added, "That would be a treat."

"We'll see later about your wish, my lady," Lia said.

"I have a few questions for Thane before he and Magni leave, Dyna. Just a moment." Eli brought over a clean gown and linen squares to wash Tamsin's face, but first she wished to hear Thane's thoughts.

As Dyna fussed with Lia, Eli asked Thane, "Where did you find her?"

"On the beach. If you look at her hands, it looks as though she climbed across the rocks. Her skin is torn. The place where we found her is craggy rocks for great lengths. He must have left her far out hoping the tide would drown her quickly, but she crawled her way to land."

Eli picked up the edge of her gown with one hand. "My guess is her knees are just as bloody."

"Can you save her?" Thane asked.

"I'll try my best. Why did she awaken?"

"Because Magni said he knows where her daughter is."

"Magni, where did you come from?"

"Ulva. The evil Garvie wished to sell us, so I stole both of us away. We hid in the bushes until I saw the chieftain and his men arrive the next morn. We were verra fortunate they came then. I knew they were safe, so I waited in his boat."

"And this happened when?"

"Late morn," Thane explained. "We were walking around our curtain wall when Magni saw a body on the beach. I never saw her. She owes her life to Magni and his good eyesight. Once I ran down to check on her, I knew she was in worst shape than the last time. As soon as Agnes got her wet clothes changed, we set out for here right away."

Maitland entered the room, closing the door quietly as he took everything in. "Magni, are you hungry yet? We have meat pies left over if you can eat one."

"A meat pie?" The lad began to cry and then asked, "For Lia too?"

Maitland saw the tub come in next and said, "I think we'll leave Lia some goat's milk while you and I search for the meat pies, unless you are anxious for a bath now." Maitland's smirk told Eli he knew exactly what the lad's response would be.

"No bath." Magni's wide eyes told them everything, and Eli did her best to contain her smile.

"Alaric, would you take Thane along? Lia is going to have a bath and some new clothes, while the lads go for food. Will that be all right with you, Lia?"

"A bath would be lovely," she whispered, that sweet smile never leaving her face. "If you please, Magni. I'll be fine here."

Magni said, "I'll have a bath later."

Thane chuckled, following Alaric and Maitland

out the door. Magni ran, telling all of them exactly how he felt about having a bath.

As soon as the door closed behind the men, Tamsin's eyes flickered open and she rolled onto her side. "Please help me save my daughter."

"We will. I promise," Eli said. "First, you must build your strength so you can tell us all you know. We cannot help her without your help."

Tamsin's gaze searched the chamber again. "Thane? He saved me again? I made it?"

Eli sat on a stool and cocooned Tamsin's hand in hers. "Aye, Thane and Magni saved you. You fought hard, but I'll help you heal so we can find your daughter."

Tamsin's eyes moved over to the tub behind Eli where Dyna was helping Lia climb into the warm water. "Alana?"

"Nay, Lia. An orphan Thane saved. But they were on Ulva. I think they can help you locate Alana. But you must heal first."

"Please help me. I don't think Alana will be alive for long. I'm certain my husband plans to sell her."

Eli jolted.

Selling bairns? What crime could be worse?

She pursed her lips and said, "You can count on our help for that. The swine is done selling bairns."

CHAPTER TWENTY-SIX

Thane

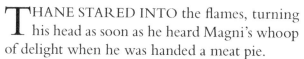

THANE STARED INTO the flames, turning his head as soon as he heard Magni's whoop of delight when he was handed a meat pie.

"My belly growled at your castle, Chief, but then we found Lady Garvie, and I forgot I was hungry."

Maitland said, "Eat it slowly, lad, or it will come back up on you. I'm guessing you have not eaten much in a while."

Magni said, "I'll try, Chief."

Thane was most interested in hearing about his sister, but he guessed she was probably asleep since it was dark already. "Mora? Is she hale? Has she been any trouble?"

"Nay," Maitland said. "Astra loves having her here. They've become fast friends and the bairns love Mora too. They all sleep in the same chamber. I love her bright outlook, but I must ask, has no one ever taught her not to ask so many questions?"

"Nay."

Maitland arched a brow and grinned.

"I do not wish to change her. I like my sister as she is. She was never allowed to ask questions until we were left alone on the isle."

Maitland rubbed his hands together. "Someday, I'd like to hear that story, but first we will focus on Tamsin." He took a goblet of ale Alaric brought for them.

Alaric sat at a trestle table and asked, "Do you and Garvie have a history, MacQuarie? Is he after you for any reason?"

Thane thought for a moment and said, "Nay. I've never met the man before this happened. Our only encounter was the day I witnessed him leave Tamsin on a rock to die. This is the second time he's left her, but I didn't see him this morn. She was already on the beach when we first saw her."

"But on the beach may not be a place to die. He is punishing her? Scaring her, possibly?" Maitland asked.

"Nay, he meant to kill her. Everyone knows it," Magni mumbled on a mouthful.

"Everyone?" Maitland's gaze narrowed as he waited for Magni to reply.

Magni chewed what was already in his mouth, then answered. "He told his guards he wished to kill his wife. He wanted a new one to give him a son, and the only way to do it was to have the first one die."

Maitland tipped his head, then glanced over at Alaric as if an agreement was forged between the two with just a look.

"The church does not allow a man to have two wives. That's what all the villagers said, but they all believe that Raghnall lives by his own rules. That he is not governed by God." Magni took another bite and sighed. "You have a fine cook."

"We do. Murreal is the wife of one of our guards. She'll be teaching others her ways."

"I'll learn!" Magni shouted.

Thane said, "We'll wait and see where you belong, Magni. Your sister needs you for now."

"Och, but this is true. Are you going to take Tamsin back?"

"That depends on Tamsin," Thane said. "She chose to return before. Her husband has their daughter, and she'll not leave her there alone. As long as their daughter remains on Ulva, I think she'll return."

"I know where Alana is. I can show you."

Maitland glanced from Alaric to Thane. "Are you sure?"

"Aye. They keep her where they kept Lia. They let me run about, gave me chores, but Lia stayed with the woman in the back building, and she's mean. She keeps the wee ones. She lives in a cottage toward the western end of the isle."

Thane thought about this revelation, wondering if he could find Alana and bring her back to Tamsin.

Alaric said, "I know what you are thinking, but I have questions for you before we make a plan."

Thane arched a brow at Alaric, wondering if his questions would be too personal. He wouldn't give away much, but he nodded his agreement. Asking didn't mean he would answer.

"What are your feelings for Tamsin? Would you accept her?" Alaric leaned back and crossed his arms while he waited.

"Accept her?"

"Are you interested in taking her for your wife?" Maitland clarified. "I think Alaric is wondering where Tamsin should live if we kill Garvie. Which is exactly what we plan to do."

"Plan? What?" So confused, he didn't know how to answer anything yet.

"Have you considered the possibility of taking Tamsin as your wife? You seem drawn to her more than as her rescuer. If I'm wrong, just say so." Maitland got up and strode over to the hearth, brushing the crumbs from his hands into the fire. He chuckled and said, "Maeve says it's a better place for the crumbs than in my beard."

"You're wrong, Chief. I'm not interested in taking a wife." Hell, the thought hadn't even crossed his mind, but Thane wasn't about to tell them the truth. He'd never take a wife.

Never. He did not trust women and all they represented. Being the only one who raises bairns, they can do what they wish with the innocent. Treat them harshly, starve them. No one pays the mothers any mind.

The only female he loved or trusted was his sister. Though he had to admit, he must trust Eli and Dyna, or he would never have left Mora with them.

Maitland sat in the large chair again, leaned

forward, placed his elbows on his knees. "My apologies. Look, MacQuarie, we know there are problems on the isle. We were warned that you have thieves and other concerns. Our job is to take care of the issues and settle the island. King Robert will not allow the MacDougalls to return here, so we must prove that we will be staying. Whoever else is causing problems will be dealt with fairly in Scotland's name. We hope to unite the island, not cause trouble."

Alaric added, "And right now, we see Garvie and his mother as problems. We'll eliminate both if necessary. We'll start with Raghnall, but if we must, we'll go after his mother. Just because she's female does not mean she is incapable of these deeds. In our experience, women can be as evil as any man. We'll investigate the chieftain and mother. And especially take a hard look at their activities."

Thane couldn't argue with them, but it changed one part of his plan. He probably wouldn't be taking over Ulva if they were involved. Are they hoping to run the isle themselves?

Or are they planning to overtake all of the Isle of Mull?

He'd be bold and ask his questions because they were paramount to his situation and his future plans. "You do know that Ulva is run by Garvie and his mother? He's driven the others out. I was told by a merchant that they come once a sennight to sell their wares, and that is it. Garvie has driven all the others off the isle. Only the ones who work directly for him remain."

Magni jumped out of his chair. "True. All true. He wants to invite others to join him."

"Who?" Maitland asked.

Magni shrugged, taking another bite of his meat pie. "I don't know. I saw another bad man there once, but I don't know who he is."

Maitland and Alaric glanced at each other again, as if thoughts passed from one to the other without words. Maitland shook his head. "We'll have to ask Tamsin if she knows Garvie's plans, when she is able."

"Is it your plan to take over the isle?" Thane asked, hoping he wasn't being too bold.

Maitland snorted. "Nay. I have a newborn son on the way. My wife will join us once she has the bairn. She wishes to have a certain healer tend to her, which is why she is staying on the mainland until she has the lad." Maitland closed his eyes. "And I miss her dearly."

Thane didn't understand this comment. He didn't know many couples who truly enjoyed each other. Clan Grantham had given him much to think on because so many of their values went against his own. Was it time to adjust the cardinal truths he held close? He thought back on his nightmare, the one where the blood flowed around his feet. Were his parents happy? Could that woman have been his mother and not his aunt? Could he be happily married?

How he wished he knew exactly what had happened so many years ago. But then the harsh truth always brought him back. His mother, the one who had raised the three of them so harshly, was not the woman in his dream. But he had no idea who she was.

Dyna exited the healing chamber and headed for their group at the hearth. Thane stood up, hoping she was bringing good news and not bad. "Is she hale?"

Dyna nodded, taking a stool next to Maitland. "She will be fine. Eli said much as last time, she has many bruises. Different from last time is the number of cuts she has, evidence of her journey across the rocks. She has one ankle that is verra swollen, but I don't think it is broken. Her walking will be limited for a while. If her husband left her as far out as she has said, then he's definitely guilty of attempted murder."

"She is coherent?" Thane asked.

"Aye. Awake, sipping on broth. She will heal, but not as fast as she hopes, I'm afraid."

"Because she will go after her husband? Or her daughter?"

"Both," Dyna said. "The only way to keep her here is to convince her that someone else will retrieve her daughter."

Magni moved over to a spot in front of the hearth and lay down, curling up and closing his eyes. Dyna covered him with a blanket. "Maitland, what say you?"

"Alaric? Have we enough trained men?"

Alaric rubbed his hands together, thinking as he stared up at the rafters. "We're still light, but what if we do a patrol first? See what we can learn? How many can you give us, MacQuarie?"

"About a score. I would ask if I could train with

you on the morrow, before I leave. I could use some new skills of my own."

"Of course. Alaric and Broc love adding newcomers to the lists. Beware," Maitland said with a laugh.

"And how many guards do you have at this point?"

Alaric replied, "We're nearing a score if we count all of us. We have another ten from the village who are training with us. I expect only half to stay, but they are strong. We can only offer a score at this point. How many MacVeys and Rankins. Have you any idea?"

Thane said, "Not exact numbers. MacVey is larger than Rankin. I'd guess Clan MacVey to be triple our size and Clan Rankin to be double. I cannot advise you as to their skill level."

The door opened and Eli entered, closing it softly behind her. She walked to Alaric, and he wrapped his arms around her, kissing her neck, and Eli squirmed. "Soon enough, Alaric." Then she turned and rubbed her bottom against him, giggling.

"Update, Eli, before you ravage your husband?" Dyna asked.

Thane thought he must have heard wrong. Eli ravage Alaric?

Eli stepped away from Alaric and said, "I will do my best to control myself. Lia and Tamsin are both asleep. I banked the fire so they should be fine." Then she leaned over and kissed her husband, tugging him close. When she ended the kiss, she leaned into him, and he wrapped his arms around her. "Now may we go?"

Dyna said, "Go. I'll show Thane and Magni to their chamber." The two raced up the stairs. Alaric grabbed her and Eli giggled as they moved.

"They are newly wed," Maitland explained. "Just as I am."

His wistful answer was clear to Thane. Both were happily married.

"Watching those two together makes me miss my wife terribly."

Thane had much to think on. He had a strict rule that his guards were to keep their wives outside the keep unless they were attacked. They stayed in cottages, and that suited Thane just fine. Everything was different at Clan Grantham. Which made him recall the question he wished to ask Dyna after Maitland took his leave to his chamber off the great hall.

Thane whispered, "How does Maitland know he's having a son?"

Dyna said, "Because I told him so." She waggled a brow at Thane and added, "I'm a seer."

Thane had much to learn about his new neighbors, but the biggest question he had was a simple one: Could he trust them?

CHAPTER TWENTY-SEVEN

Tamsin

TAMSIN STOOD IN the gloomy morn, doing her best to ignore the two lassies in front of her who could fire their arrows as fast as anyone she'd ever seen.

"How old are they again?"

"Five and almost four," Dyna replied. "My wee lassies are fierce!"

Tora said, "Mama, watch me. I'm the best."

"Nay, you are not," Sylvi argued. "I am. See, Mama?" The resounding whacks rang out as their arrows hit the hay at the end of their area.

"Astra, take the girls out in search of berries. I need to work with Tamsin alone."

"Aww …" The two voices rose in unison.

Soon after, Sylvi said, "I'll beat you there, Tora."

"Always competing, those two. Tamsin, wait until they are gone. Then I'll work on your stance. Grab something to drink. I'll be right back once I get the girls settled."

Tamsin made her way over to the well off to the side of the courtyard, finding a cup to fill with water before dropping it back into the bucket when she finished. The light lilt of a lass's giggling caught her ear.

Eli and Alaric strolled across the courtyard and out to the lists, if she were to guess, because Eli called out, "I think you need your tunic removed before you can truly swing that sword, husband."

Alaric whipped off his tunic and tossed it to her. "And do you wish for me to remove my plaid too? There are not many around." He tipped his head toward the outer edge where a copse of trees sat. "We can do a fast one, if you like, lassie mine. You first, this time."

Tamsin had no idea what that meant, but she sat on a hidden bench, listening to their conversation, unable to believe all she heard.

"I like it when you pick me up and hold me where you want me. That's the only way, Alaric. Lift me onto you behind the trees or wait until this eve." She glanced over at him. "The weather is mighty fine." She removed her leggings and carried them over her shoulder, then wiggled her bottom at him.

Tamsin was shocked at their behavior, and there was no one around but her to witness their foreplay.

"And where shall I bang hard at you? You only like it hard." He chuckled as Tamsin peeked over at them again.

"Against the wall. If you don't hit me too hard. Hold my upper body still and ram my spot hard." She giggled. "Hard and fast, lover. You know how I like it."

Tamsin was glad they couldn't see how her eyes widened at that. They had to be talking about something different from what she thought. How could they have relations standing up? And Eli had definitely said she liked it.

Liked it?

And as a complete surprise, the two took off into the trees to do whatever they had planned. Within minutes, their mutual sounds of pleasure reached Tamsin's ears. Alaric sounded much like Raghnall, except for his kind words.

"Come for me, love."

"Scream my name, lass."

"Eli, squeeze me."

But the oddest thing happened, something she didn't understand. Eli panted as much as Alaric did. And her words carried as well.

"Touch me. You know where."

"Finish this!"

"More, more."

"Harder!"

"Faster!"

"Oh, Alaric!"

Then a roar and a scream rent the air, both indicating their pleasure.

Dyna appeared in front of her, a wide grin on her face.

Tamsin blushed, and she was glad she was unable to see herself or she'd be more mortified. Caught eavesdropping on a lovemaking session was something she thought would never happen.

Never.

But the oddest part of it was that it was truly

a lovemaking session. Eli had expressed her pleasure in such a guttural, soul-ripping way that Tamsin couldn't help but wonder how it had felt. It sounded as though Eli had enjoyed it.

Could the act be pleasurable for a woman too?

"I'll apologize for Eli and Alaric." Dyna sat down and shook her head. "They are one of those couples who enjoy their lovemaking so much that they do it often. More often than most of us, and they have no shame. They do not care who hears them, and they perform as often outside as they do inside. I have to make up stories for my bairns as to what they are doing. Once I blamed it on tree-climbing. Another time I said Eli got stuck on the well pump. I was quite fond of that one."

Alaric and Eli came across the courtyard toward the well, Eli squealing because Alaric had carried her over his shoulder, and she giggled ecstatically, her hands grabbing his bottom under his plaid and squeezing. "I'll wash you up, sweeting." But then Alaric caught sight of the two of them and spun on his heels to take her to the stables instead. Eli never noticed them.

Tamsin couldn't take her eyes from the couple. She whispered, "They truly love each other, don't they?"

Dyna sighed. "They do. How old are you?"

"Eight and ten."

"So, you've never been in love, have you?"

Tamsin shook her head. "My sire chose my husband. I never met him until our wedding day. I didn't know—"

"That coupling could be enjoyable for both? It should be, if the man has any consideration in him."

"It is not painful for you?" All Tamsin could think of was how Raghnall forced her legs apart and ripped into her like a bull.

"If done correctly, the woman has secretions to ease his way. There is a spot that can give the woman pleasure. And sometimes, I like it even if I don't orgasm because we are so close. Like we fit so well that we were made for each other. Makes me realize how we belong together."

"Orgasm?"

"When a woman or a man finds their pleasure, they call it an orgasm. Someday when you find the right man, you will understand. Desire can be powerful. A good husband will find your pleasure spot for you."

"Raghnall does not care about me."

"Or anyone else but himself, I would guess. You will not be married to him much longer."

Tamsin stared at her new friend, wishing to ask how she could be so sure, but Dyna stood, ending the discussion. "Come, we have archery lessons to learn. I'll tell you about the woman who taught me. Eli's grandmother, Gwyneth Ramsay. She once shot a man between his bollocks, pinning him to the tree by his sac."

Tamsin couldn't hide her gasp. "What did he do?"

"He dared to touch her daughter and niece. Hid them from her, which is why she didn't kill him outright. She needed information. He gave it to her once he was pinned to the tree."

"Did he survive?"

"Nay. Died with his hands on his bollocks, dripping with blood."

Tamsin envisioned Dyna's story, shocked by this admission. "He kidnapped the girls?"

"Aye, kidnapped them and locked them away. They'd been with him for days. Gwyneth and Logan were not happy. It was something to see, so I was told."

"He deserved it if he hurt bairns."

"Indeed he did. There have been many tales about that day. It's a vision that makes men cover their private area with their hands. Kind of entertaining to tell it."

Tamsin could envision it, but the man had a different face—Raghnall's.

"Teach me. I can learn."

"I'd be happy to do that. But I have another question for you. Did your mother never talk to you about men?"

She shook her head. "My mother died when I was young. My sister and I were raised by our father. He didn't talk much. Left the hut to hunt in the morn and returned in the eve, expecting to have everything the way it was when Mama was alive. He was not a happy man." She didn't expand on the worst parts of the story.

"Where is your sister now? And is she older or younger?"

"A year younger. Her name is Meg, and I have

no idea where she is. I've not seen my family since I was forced to marry Raghnall."

"I'm sorry to hear that, but I'm going to be verra blunt because I'm guessing your father never taught you the one skill every lass needs to know."

Puzzled, Tamsin held her breath because she had no idea what Dyna was about to tell her, but by instinct, she knew it was important. "I'm listening."

"Did you know that hurting a man in his bollocks will cause so much pain that it will drop him to his knees?"

"What?" She'd never heard of such a thing.

"You can kick them between their legs, punch them, and if they are trying to force themselves on you, take their sac in your hands and squeeze. They'll be powerless to hurt you, and it will give you time to get away."

Tamsin wished to scream to the world. Why had no one told her such a thing? She could have stopped the times Raghnall had forced himself on her?

"A word of warning."

"Aye?"

"Make sure you hit them in the right place, and you have a plan to escape, because they will not like it. It's extremely painful. A man like Raghnall will retaliate with his fists, multiple times. But he will be frozen until you get away. But you better run fast."

She could definitely run faster than Raghnall.

CHAPTER TWENTY-EIGHT

Thane

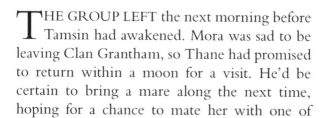

THE GROUP LEFT the next morning before Tamsin had awakened. Mora was sad to be leaving Clan Grantham, so Thane had promised to return within a moon for a visit. He'd be certain to bring a mare along the next time, hoping for a chance to mate her with one of their fine stallions.

The group was larger than he'd expected because Maitland had decided to come along with Eli and Alaric to patrol Ulva. Maitland had insisted. "It's not just about Ulva. You are traveling with three bairns, though Mora is hardly young, but she is a beauty. You need more protection." Thane hadn't argued with one of the chieftains of Clan Grantham.

Lia rode with Eli and Magni rode with Thane. Mora rode her own horse, her new bow and quiver attached to her saddle. Maitland had also brought two more guards along. With Brian and Artan and his guards, they now numbered over a dozen.

Thane led the way over the most common path but planned to bring them into the rear of his land instead of following the coastline. They could take their leave either way, but he wished to show his new allies how to reach his castle more quickly.

He had a feeling he didn't like, and it proved to be true.

As he came down the last path to his curtain wall, he had a wide view of the water, the advantage of living in a castle on a hill above the sea. It gave them a clear view of two boats headed toward shore, directly in front of his castle, and if he had to guess, he'd wager it to be Garvie and his men. He often saw fishing boats in the cove in front of his land, but rarely birlinns.

Alaric had also spotted the men from their higher vantage point, off to the side of Thane's castle. "Friend or enemy?" he asked Thane.

"Not friends. My guess is they are coming from Ulva, but I know not where they are headed."

"Get the bairns inside, then we'll go around front and determine their purpose," Maitland said. "Do you have a back door through your curtain wall?"

"Aye," he said, pointing.

"How many guards are here to protect the castle?"

"Nearly a score. I don't have a full line of soldiers yet. We're still building."

"It is Garvie," Magni announced, his arms flying over his head in frustration. "Those are his ships. His flag. Please don't let him take us back!"

Lia said, "Fear not, brother. I am confident our new friends will protect us."

Thane was often taken aback by the maturity of the lass's thoughts and vocabulary. He had grown men in his guard who didn't speak that clearly.

Magni looked from Thane to Maitland and asked, "Is she right, Chief? Will you protect us? Please?" The fear in the poor lad's voice had caught all of them.

Alaric said, "They'll not touch either of you, Magni."

"Nay, they will not," Thane echoed.

Magni's response was to turn around and hug Thane. "We will stay with you forever."

"Does he attack often, Magni?" Alaric asked.

"He has no friends, so he only leaves to attack someone who doesn't do what he orders or to meet someone to sell the bairns to. They usually come from Europe. I know not where that is." Magni looked from chieftain to chieftain.

Thane sighed. "I need to know what he's about. You all go inside, and I'll creep around to listen. See what they have planned."

Eli said, "We'll go with you."

"Brian, take the bairns into the keep."

Magni shouted, "I'll go with you! I can hear him from far away. But please take my sister where she'll be safe."

"Fine, but hush for now, Magni." Lia gave the boy a stern look, as if she were the parent.

The group separated, Brian and Maitland going inside with two guards, Lia, and Mora, while the other two guards remained with Thane. Once the departing group was within the curtain wall, Thane turned to lead his group to a different path, but he picked up another noise.

They all heard the same sound, and Eli fired two arrows in rapid succession, a big buck falling not far from them.

"Nice shot, Eli," Alaric said with a grin. "Good eating this eve."

Thane couldn't believe his eyes. He'd barely heard the buck, but Eli had arranged herself and fired before the buck knew they were there. Hell, but he had to learn how to use a bow. His mouth watered at the thought of smoking all that meat. They'd eat well for a moon or more.

Alaric and Artan moved to retrieve the deer, getting it almost to the curtain wall when another sound interrupted them.

Six men came out of the woods, four on horseback. One said, "Get the lass."

Alaric nearly spewed, his fury visible on his face instantaneously. "Like hell. Try to get near her, you bastards."

Eli fired three arrows so fast that Thane could barely follow them in the air, but two found their targets, dropping two men off their mounts, the third arrow just missing.

Alaric hadn't unsheathed his sword but reached for his bow instead, firing along with Eli. Another arrow came from the curtain wall, and Thane looked up, surprised to see Mora up on top, firing. She hit a man's leg—he yelped, so Thane went after him to finish him off.

The attack only lasted minutes because several of the marauders ran in the opposite direction, not wanting to battle against the archers. Two were dead, and one wounded, but he'd been carried away by another of his peers.

Once they were gone, Alaric asked, "Who were they? And what lass were they after? I can't believe they wanted Eli. I thought we'd taken care of all those fools on Ramsay land."

"I heard one say the lass had disappeared. Mayhap they were after Lia or Mora." Thane scanned the area for any more attackers before leaving. "We can discuss this later. For now, I need to see what activity is taking shape up front. My first goal is to ascertain if Garvie is on the ship and if his intent is to come here. I'll leave my horse. Artan, you stay back."

"I'm coming," Magni said.

Thane put his fingers to his lips as he moved Magni behind him, creeping along toward the coastline. He kept close to the curtain wall while Alaric and Eli followed, armed with their bows. Once they were close enough to listen and see the two ships, Thane knelt down, motioning for the others to hide in a nearby copse of bushes.

Voices carried across the water as if they were two horse-lengths away. Garvie said, "I'm going to end this slime's life and take his castle. This location is a better place to meet boats instead of on Ulva. We can have a much larger operation. He can't have more than a score total, and we have ten more than that. The element of surprise will be in our favor."

"Aye, Chief," one man said. "What about the bairns?"

"I want the yellow-haired lass. The lad disappeared, but I had a good deal for a five-winters-old who was that fine. I don't know if she is here, but if you see her, bring her to me."

Another asked, "Shall we look for your wife?"

"Nay. Do not bother. If she's here, I don't want the bitch back. I hope she's dead by now."

Thane closed his eyes for a second, the words he'd just heard too painful. The man was sheer evil. Raghnall Garvie only cared about himself and whatever coin he could get.

Alaric whispered to him, "We can send them back into their ships. They have paltry weapons. A few arrows will have them scampering to their boats and rowing for their lives. Men like that are not used to dealing with archers."

Thane thought for a moment and said, "Do it. It sounds like they are after Lia and my castle. They'll get neither one."

Magni said, "I need a dagger. I can sneak down and stick it in his black heart, the snarly creep. He'll not get my sister." The lad held his fist up and waved it at the man.

"You'll stay here. You and I will watch Eli and Alaric and hope the ships set for Ulva quickly. If we have to, we'll assist by using our swords if any approach the castle. Until then, we will observe and listen only."

The husband-and-wife pair put on quite a show, firing six arrows in rapid succession. The men did just what Alaric had predicted. They ran and squealed like lasses as soon as the first man took an arrow to his shoulder.

But it wasn't Garvie they hit. He hid behind all his men the moment the first arrow landed. "Get your oars! Get in position! We must leave quickly." The fool's voice carried to them easily over the shouts of his men.

Magni began to giggle, and Thane put his hand over his mouth. But the more they watched, the more he giggled. Thane joined him.

After two more arrows, Alaric turned around and said to Thane, "That answers our question. When we decide to attack his men on the island, it will be over in no time. The men have no bollocks and no weapons."

Magni giggled again. "They have no bollocks at all. They are a bunch of girls." The last word came out in a long lilt.

Eli gave him a hard stare and whispered, "What's wrong with girls?"

"Naught! I'm sorry. Forgive me. You know I love girls. I love Lia and Mora and you, my lady."

"That's better." Eli aimed again, a small smile on her face.

Thane had to stand up for the poor lad. "The only girls he has known are his sister and mean ones. The isle doesn't have many."

"Those men are like rats. Ugly rats. They run away as soon as they see someone." Magni began to laugh at his own jest. His giggle turned into a guffaw, and the boat stopped momentarily as if they'd heard the lad, but Eli fired two more arrows, then their rowing resumed.

Magni got up to head toward the castle, but Thane put a hand on him. "Not until they are nearly on Ulva. I do not trust them at all."

Magni said, "I'll watch for you, Chief. I can be the one who watches the shore every morning for ships and bodies both. I'll work hard. I promise." Magni stared across the water again. "Do you think they'll be back?"

Thane had been considering that possibility, but he didn't let on. "Nay, they're afraid of archers. You never saw any on Ulva, did you?"

Magni shook his head, still watching the departing ships.

Thane turned back to Alaric and said, "What the hell do they want with the lasses?"

Magni looked up at Thane. "I have to protect Lia. Please, promise me we can stay here with you, Chief? I don't want to be in the woods again. If we'd been in the woods together, they would have stolen her away."

Thane nodded, taking in all their surroundings before going in through the front gates, across the bridge. "I think they're gone for now. I will protect you and your sister, Magni. Do not worry."

Alaric asked, "No moat in the back?"

"Nay. Only in the front where it was easy to dig. The back needs too many trees removed. We didn't have the manpower, but it does deter those who come from the beach."

Thane said, "I hope you'll stay this eve. I could use your guidance on how to proceed from here. Should I go for Alana and bring her to Tamsin? Or should I wait for more men?"

"We'll see what Maitland thinks. He is the best strategist. He and Dyna have the experience we lack."

Alaric and Maitland helped Thane with the deer Eli had taken down, swearing it was enough to feed his men for a long time. They'd had a lovely pottage to start, taking a bit of the meat to simmer while they set the rest up for smoking. Thane had a great firepit behind his castle, and they'd enjoyed a night of camaraderie.

When they were around the fire, it was Maitland who asked, "Have you any idea who the first attackers were? Could they have been men sent by Garvie to attack from behind?"

Thane considered this for a moment before he answered. "I don't think so. We've been here for about four years, took the castle over after it was deserted. A fire had damaged it enough that the owners felt it wasn't worth salvaging, apparently. There were six of us to start, but once Artan joined us, we grew into a solid group. We dedicated our time to fishing, hunting, and repairing the damage done. It took a while, but we used stone mostly, and our efforts have paid off."

"How many times have you been attacked?" Alaric asked.

"Never. We are isolated and most think it's still damaged on the inside, is my guess. There are fishermen about, but we don't see many. Artan took us to Tobermory a few times for supplies, but we cut our own wood and use the stone we find in the forest. He's taught us about growing grain and some vegetables, but mostly we forage and fish."

"How many men?"

"If we had to battle, mayhap a dozen could fight. We bought swords, and I trained with a man in Tobermory and brought back what I could, but we could definitely use more sword skills. And we would benefit highly from archers. It makes hunting much easier than using spears. We eat more fish than meat, which is why we are grateful for any deer."

"Who else would have attacked you, then?" Alaric asked.

"I honestly don't have any idea. They had no identifiable plaids, so I don't think they were from Clan MacVey or Clan Rankin. Is there a new group on the isle? But I have another question for all of you because we heard it from Garvie and from the men. Why do they want the girl? And which one? Mora or Lia?"

"Or Eli?" Maitland asked.

Eli snorted and Alaric choked, finally saying with a grin, "See how they do with that. I don't know how they'll die quicker, by my hand or hers."

Eli drawled, "I can tell you which death will be more painful …"

Maitland chuckled, but then replied, "I don't think they want Eli. They want Mora or Lia, but I don't know why. There are many reasons they could want either one."

Eli said what they all feared. "Or both."

Were they looking for a specific lass or any they could find?

CHAPTER TWENTY-NINE

Eli

THANKS TO FINE weather, Eli, Alaric, and Maitland returned to Duart Castle the next day. There was still much to do to get their castle functioning the way it should if they wished to attract members to join Clan Grantham.

Mora had been sad to see them leave, but she'd become quite fond of Lia and Magni. True to her nature, her parting words had been, "Many thanks for allowing me to visit with Astra. Do you think she will stay for a while? Could I visit again? Mayhap around Yuletide? Will you tell the bairns I miss them?"

Eli hugged her tightly and said, "Aye to all. We will see you often. Do not despair, lass. You are part of our extended family now." That brought tears to Mora's eyes.

And now she understood Mora better. When they'd relaxed around the hearth after the evening meal, Thane had told them how the three had been raised, and how their mother had left them on the beach when Mora had been seven. He had explained how they'd repaired the castle from fire damage and had grown in numbers also.

Maitland had quietly stated, "If you ever find the woman again, I'd be pleased to meet her. Tell her my thoughts of how she treated her own bairns."

The look in Maitland's eyes told all, but Maitland had explained, "My first wife and I lost a bairn, so apparently, she doesn't understand their value. I'd like to explain it to her."

As Eli's father once told her, there were often reasons for things that you'll never know until afterward. Mora had needed to be around more females, and they had needed to help Clan MacQuarie.

When they came down the main path from Craignure, Eli had been surprised to see more of the cottages in the village now occupied. They'd been deserted when they'd arrived, but now half of them were full. People came out to greet them, and Maitland stopped to introduce himself. Alaric invited several men to join the guards, if they were interested.

Once they arrived back at Duart Castle, they were pleased to see that Derric had found a goat herder nearby who he'd contracted with for a daily delivery of milk, a smithy who was looking for work, and a woman from the village who agreed to come in the morning and set their food for the midday meal.

Life was returning to Duart Castle.

Most surprising was to find Dyna working

with Tamsin in the archery field. Eli applauded but then headed inside the castle.

Once they'd had a small repast, Maitland said, "I'm going back to the village to recruit more guards. I wish to see how many are there, who wishes to plant, and anything else I can learn. With all these new tenants, we could use a nice deer to have a feast in a couple of days. Feel like hunting, you two?" He grinned and took his leave.

Alaric said, "He makes a solid point. We could use the meat. We have the ability to smoke whatever we don't eat, and I look forward to a feast for the new villagers."

"I must find someone who can bake. But meat comes first, so I'll go."

"I challenge you. Who can bring back the largest prey, bird or animal. Though I do not mind losing to my beautiful wife, I must be able to hit a rabbit, at the very least."

Eli laughed and grabbed his arm, tugging him along. "I say we go now. I could change my tunic, but I'll change after we hunt."

The two rode together to leave the horses for the others.

"I'm enjoying the fish, Eli. We could go to the loch, if you'd prefer." Alaric flicked the reins toward the forest.

Eli was accustomed to Alaric's teasing. She never tried to hide that she preferred meat to fish, though a nice salmon was sweet at times. "Meat, husband. You know how much I love meat."

He snorted. "And I'm glad of it."

She threw her head back and laughed. But then she became serious. "I've had enough trout. The fishing is fine here, but the deer meat we had at Thane's was delicious. Could the red stag be tastier than the typical Highland deer meat? Either way, it was a tease to my taste buds. I need a big stag of our own, Alaric. But what am I looking for exactly? What else besides deer? I didn't see any boar on our journey."

"Maitland said mostly red deer. He did mention pheasant. Eagles, osprey, rabbit, duck, mayhap geese."

"No boar?"

"He didn't mention it, and we have not seen any yet. Mayhap you'll see one."

"I'm hoping for a big fat pheasant or a deer."

"Duck, straight ahead," he whispered.

She fired but missed. "Bloody hell and a hedgehog."

Several moments later, Alaric slowed his horse. "Deer ahead. A big stag."

"I see it," she whispered. Eli climbed off the horse, Alaric helping her to drop silently as she held her bow with one hand, her quiver across her back. She would not lose sight of the beast. They needed that meat.

She fired one arrow but missed, the deer only moving slightly, turning its head toward her.

"Come on," she whispered. "Give me the broad side, big lad. Easier to hit." She waited, holding her breath, for just the right shot. Before she loosed her shot, another arrow crossed her path.

She ignored it, doing what she had to do. She let hers go and caught the stag, dropping him.

But she couldn't forget what she'd seen. A moment later, another arrow passed in front of her eyes, not close, but close enough.

She dropped her bow. "What the hell?"

"Eli, someone is shooting at us. Get back here!"

But something caught her. She was close enough to the arrow to know she recognized that fletching. She followed the path of the arrow until she found it lying in a bush.

"You witchin' bitch! I know who you are!" She took off running straight at the source of the arrow, in the opposite direction of Alaric and their horse. Two more came at her and went wide.

"Eli, wait!"

She ignored him, too focused on her prey at the moment, and they would not escape her this time.

"Eli, arms up. I'm coming for you." Alaric's voice came from a distance behind her.

She heard him, but didn't stop, instead running as fast as she could. She'd not lose them this time. The pounding of the hooves behind her shook the ground and when he was nearly upon her, she stopped and held her arms over her head moments before Alaric bent down to grasp her waist and sweep her onto the horse in front of him.

Eli landed with an oof, but she was still furious. Furious and elated—but which emotion was more powerful? "It's her, Alaric. I'd know her fletching anywhere."

"Your grandmother? Are you sure?"

Two more arrows came toward them from a copse of trees ahead, but both went wide.

"Eli, whoever it is has a different intent than you think. Are you daft? They're trying to kill us. I'm turning around."

Eli nearly grabbed the reins but instead she said, "Nay, husband. She's missing on purpose. Those arrows are so far away from us, the person should be ashamed, but it is intentional. I know her. She'd not shoot at us. It was Grandpapa I saw the other day. They're here. I swear it. And I want to know why!"

Nearly on top of their target, two more arrows went wider than before.

"Stop shooting, Grandmama! Logan Ramsay, stop her from shooting!" She yelled at the top of her lungs, making sure they heard her. She would not turn around.

The arrows stopped, and they neared the trees, so she hopped down and ran straight into them.

Her grandfather stood to the side of a boulder where her grandmother sat with a large blanket on her lap.

"You were shooting at us! You were! I saw you. Are you trying to kill your own granddaughter? What the hell?" She ran straight for her grandfather and shoved him in the chest.

He didn't try to stop her, the look of admiration nearly dropping her to the ground. Then that wee smirk of his.

Then she turned to her grandmother. "How could you? I've thought you dead all this time and here you are, better than ever." She moved to grab the bow out of her grandmother's hand. "Give me that. How dare you shoot at us? What the hell is wrong with you? Have you gone daft?"

When she yanked the bow away, the blanket came with it.

First Eli gasped at what was revealed underneath, then she fell on her grandmother, sobbing her eyes out. "Grandmama, I've missed you so much."

CHAPTER THIRTY

Eli

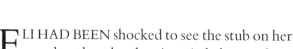

ELI HAD BEEN shocked to see the stub on her grandmother, her legging tied above where her knee would have been on one leg. That explained why she sat on a boulder shooting instead of firing from a tree. She'd had part of her leg amputated.

She hugged her dear grandmother, then climbed off the rock and lunged at her dear grandfather, still sobbing. "Why didn't you tell me? And why the hell were you shooting at us? You know our plaid."

Gwyneth Ramsay said, "Not his fault, Eli. I was confused. You know I don't see well. I thought it was a Rankin plaid."

"You are full of the shite of the biggest bull in all the land with that comment, Grandmama," she said, standing and placing her hands on her hips. "Why are you lying so?"

Alaric came up behind her, his hands settling on her shoulders, then he leaned over and said,

"Remember the one thing you've wished for more than anything? You have it. Do not lose it."

And she leaned back into his heat, his arms wrapping around her and holding her tight. She whispered, "Must you always be right, husband?"

Then Alaric asked, "Why the secrecy, Logan?"

"Come over here."

Her grandmother patted the spot next to her on the boulder, so Eli sat down. "I don't understand."

Her grandfather sat on a log and said, "We were hired to come here and see who is causing all the issues. Cattle-stealing shouldn't take place on an island where there are so few cattle. King Robert wants to know if there are MacDougalls still causing trouble or what. With Gwynie's problem, it was a good time to take our leave. It was to be done in secret, and you are not to share this with anyone but Maitland and Dyna."

"So why didn't you tell me? Why not stay with us? You could visit and spy without telling us."

Her grandfather looked to her grandmother, but she lifted her chin higher, the stubborn nature more than evident at the moment. "Grandmama, why?"

The pause was longer than the shadows in a forest at twilight, but she would wait for her answer. "All right. Have you not seen my leg? It was lose my leg or die, so I had no choice, but I wish for my reputation to stand tall. I want my legacy as the best archer in all the land to remain. If anyone sees me like this, I will look like a cripple and my reputation will crumble. I want …" Then the tears started.

Eli wrapped her arms around this woman who had taught her so much in life. "Grandmama …"

"I'm not finished yet. I hope that my reputation will continue to make men fear our daughters and granddaughters. I wish to maintain the reputation of shooting a man in the bollocks to make any man fear my granddaughters. I can no longer protect you, but my reputation could." The tears rolled down her face freely, something Eli had never seen before.

Her grandfather said, "Elisant, it was a difficult surgery, extremely painful, as has been the healing process. She wishes you to only have memories of how strong she is. She's the strongest, most beautiful woman I've ever met, and I respect her wishes in this."

Eli rested her head on her grandmother's shoulder. "But you are so much more than your reputation, Grandmama. You are much more than Gwyneth Ramsay to me. You are my strength, and I need you. Especially in this new life. Please do not hide from me. I'll keep your secret, but can I not visit with you both? I need you, especially on the Isle of Mull."

She kissed her dear grandmother's wet cheek and then looked at her grandfather. "Do you know how much my heart ached after you left me?"

"We left everyone, not just you, lass," her grandfather said. "And our hearts ached for all of you."

"But it felt like you left me on my wedding. Duart Castle is huge and well made. Maitland

and Derric just returned with supplies. We have extra bedchambers so you can stay with us. You can stay in a comfortable bed, Grandmama."

Grandmama patted her arm. "We have a nice bed. I am healing well. Every day is better."

"Will you two promise not to hide from me? I am the only Ramsay here, so no one else is going to be searching for you."

Eli stood and glanced from one grandparent to the other, the two peeking at each other, the subtle nod finally coming from her grandmother.

Grandsire said, "We promise to visit with you once a sennight. Will that suit you? We do have work to do. And we will come when the guards are away."

"Where are you staying?"

"That is for our knowledge only at this point. When we have discovered what our king needs to know, then we will gladly stay with you for a while."

"Promise? Both of you?"

"Promise," Grandsire said, Grandmama repeating the same.

Her grandmother beckoned her back, so Eli sat down, and Grandmama kissed her forehead and said, "So proud of you and what you are building here on the Isle of Mull."

"Many thanks to you. I learned from the best."

Her grandfather said, "You are not going to find many boar here, lass, just pheasant, duck, goose, rabbit, and deer. And aye, she was shooting to miss you. Hoped to scare you off, but my granddaughter does not scare easily, does she?"

"Nay, I'd know her fletchings anywhere."

"Let's go back, Logan," Grandmother said, pushing herself to the edge of the boulder.

Eli looked at Alaric and pointed to her grandmother. He moved over to lift her, but Grandsire was there first.

"Logan Ramsay, do not touch. Let the young one do it for a change. I'll break your back soon enough."

"Gwynie, you weigh as much as a twig now." But Eli noticed the man didn't argue, instead climbing onto his horse.

Alaric lifted her onto their mount in front of her husband, her arm wrapped around his, and they were off.

Eli called out after them, "One sennight. You promised!"

CHAPTER THIRTY-ONE

Tamsin

TAMSIN STOOD IN front of the loch, taking in the beautiful view. She'd been here for four days, and her ankle was much improved. Eli had said it wasn't broken but sprained. She wouldn't be running anywhere, but she got around without too much pain, though she'd learned long ago how to function, with or without pain. Her entire being bubbled with something unfamiliar, happiness and hope. Others might think it was the blue sky or the shimmering water, but that wasn't the part she believed was the best.

It was the bairns.

Derric and Dyna were in the water with their three bairns, the wee ones kicking and squealing with delight, splashing water and jumping about as if they'd never been wet before.

"Tamsin, come in! The water is actually quite warm. Warmer than our loch in the Highlands," Dyna shouted to her.

"It looks enticing. I'm considering joining you." She was. Seriously. If there was anything she wished to learn, it was how to swim. After nearly dying twice in deep water, it was paramount that she learn how to swim.

"Would you like me to join you? I'd be happy to show you some easy maneuvers in the water." The voice came from behind her.

Tamsin jumped, whirling around, surprised to see Thane approaching from the area where they'd left their horses. She gave him a swift hug because she was glad to see him. He'd saved her twice, and she hadn't adequately expressed her appreciation for the second time.

Her arms wrapped around his neck and inhaled his scent of pine and horse, so much different from Raghnall. Tall and hard in most places, his chest felt like the side of a wall. His belly was also flat and solid.

Unlike Raghnall's moving midsection.

Thane's hands were soft and kind, and his hair was always clean, something else very different from her husband. She stepped back and blushed. "Forgive me for my forwardness. I wasn't thinking."

Thane brushed a stray hair from her face and said, "That makes the hug even better."

"Why are you here?" she asked, hoping Mora and Brian were well. "Is something wrong?"

"Nay, naught specific. We've heard tales of Garvie attacking different places, and we still have not discovered who the second group was who attacked us, but we've heard gossip about both situations. I decided I'd feel better if the three young ones were here."

"Three?" she asked, tipping her head.

"Mora, Lia, and Magni."

She had a vague memory of two other bairns coming along on their last trip, but she didn't recall actually meeting them. "I look forward to making their acquaintance. Where are they from? And do they live with you or are they visiting?"

"Magni found my boat on Ulva and decided to attempt to get away from there. He and his sister were to be sold, but he escaped from the mean old woman's place, as he called her, and found me. They'll stay with us for as long as they'd like."

"So he might know where Alana is held?"

"He claims to know. We shall use his knowledge when the time comes."

Tamsin sighed, knowing she wasn't in a position to make any demands. She would learn how to swim, practice her archery, then ask her new friends how they would suggest getting Alana back. "You also mentioned you were attacked by an unknown group? When did this happen?"

"When we returned to our land, a small group came upon us in the forest, looking for a specific lass. We have yet to determine who they were or whom they sought. I thought to ask Maitland if he has any new information about that. He seems to be the one who ferrets out tales of the isle. More than we ever hear."

"My lord, I hope I have not caused any trouble to fall upon your clan. It was certainly not my intent." She would feel horrible if Raghnall attacked Thane's clan. Had her husband attacked other clans? Not to her knowledge, but then again, she knew little of his activities outside their home.

"Not my lord, but Thane…" He brushed the back of his hand across her cheek, his touch so gentle she nearly grabbed his hand to hold it there.

She blushed and said, "Thane. I'm sorry if my husband is bothering you."

"It is not your fault. It is your husband's. He does not wish to get along with any neighbors, but instead prefers to make demands. I am not worried about Garvie." Thane glanced past her shoulder and smiled.

"They are enjoying themselves." Tamsin's heart swelled watching the loving interaction within the family, wondering how it would feel to have a husband who truly loved their bairn, and one who was kind. Derric and Dyna were wonderful parents. Tamsin often envisioned Alana playing with their wee ones.

Dyna hollered over the din of the bairns' happiness. "Come join us, both of you. How do you fare, Thane?"

"I'm well. I saw your horses here, so I thought to check on your activities."

"The water is lovely. Talk Tamsin into joining us. Though I'll warn you to keep your distance, Tamsin. Derric has naught on."

Fortunately, Derric was in deep water, so he gave no hint to being in the nude. Dyna turned back to her group, so Thane took Tamsin's elbow and said, "I'm guessing you were hoping to learn how to swim. I'd be happy to help in any way I can."

Tamsin looked into his eyes, the kindness even visible there, something she truly loved about Thane. "I was hoping to learn a bit, but they are busy with their bairns."

"Do you trust me? I could try to teach you to float on your back. That would be a great start. When in trouble, floating on your back will keep your head above water, and after that, the next skill to learn would be kicking your feet to move you to your target."

Tamsin kneaded her hands in front of her, wiggling her thumbs. She'd worn a short tunic and leggings to swim in, something Eli had suggested and shared with her so she wouldn't worry about her clothing. It was time for her to be bold and stop hiding from the world as she'd learned to do in Ulva.

"I'd welcome your assistance, Thane. Of course, I trust you. You have saved me twice, though I am unsure if I thanked you for the last time? If not, I will thank you now."

He held out his hand. "You are welcome. Come and feel the water. Your clothing is fine, but we should both remove our boots and hose."

She giggled and held on to him while she did as he suggested, her toes wiggling in the grass as he waited for her to finish before removing his own. The long grass was cool and refreshing on her feet. Someone had cut a path across the area closest to the water to make it easier to swim or fish.

Thane removed his tunic and said, "I'm glad I wore trews."

Then she peered up at him and said, "I'm ready. Please hold on to me."

"I promise never to let you go," he said, an odd feeling coursing through him when he spoke the words.

Thane took her hand in his and led her to the edge of the loch, the sun peeking out through scattered clouds as they approached, the warmth making the impending dip even more appealing. "I'm nervous," she whispered.

"I'm not surprised after all you've been through. You must always be careful about the area you enter, making sure it is as shallow as you need or deep enough for a jump. Every loch is different."

"And what about this one?"

"Derric and Dyna chose well. This section of the edge is quite shallow, perfect for wee ones to swim in so they can touch the bottom. It is mostly flat too. Many areas can have a quick drop-off, so always test it out to be certain."

They reached the edge, and something brought her hairs upright, the quick twinge traveling through her, a shiver coming unbidden. She shook it off along with the images of her husband moving her out of a boat. Her body whirled away from Thane, but she turned back to him, fighting the images in her mind.

"I'm here," he whispered. "I'll not desert you."

Her eyes misted because his words were true. "Many thanks."

"It will be cool at first, but I think we will warm to it." They stopped as soon as the water touched her toes and he said, "Go ahead. Take a step in."

She stuck one foot in and squealed, but then put the other foot in, wiggling her toes again. "It feels refreshing, Thane. Join me?"

He did, but then he surprised her, taking four large steps in before letting her hand go. "You'll be fine. I'll be right back."

Tamsin watched Thane duck into the water, going up to his shoulders before turning back to face her as he treaded across the bank to see how deep the water was, if she were to guess.

"This is perfect. Walk forward to me and once you are wet, I'll help you float."

Tamsin froze, her gaze locked on his chest, the dark hairs moving about in the water. Thane was a handsome man with a finely chiseled body. The span of his shoulders was double her husband's. Thane's thick muscles were bigger than she'd ever seen. His hair grazed the water at his shoulders, dipping and curling with the water's movement. He was as handsome as any she'd met, the slight scruff of his beard from traveling something she found attractive.

Dyna broke her focus because she called out, "Best of luck, Tamsin. You'll love it once you learn to swim. Take that power from Garvie so he'll not try it again." She loped up the bank, one bairn in each hand. "Turn your back so Derric can get out. We've been in long enough, though they'd stay in all day if we'd allow it."

Tamsin turned toward Thane and waved to the group as they left. "Tell me what to do next, Thane." She had to concentrate, listen to his instructions, and ignore his chest. That was her only choice at present. She was still married, though she would officially end their marriage if she could do it. For this moment, she'd allow herself to dream that Thane belonged to her, that they were married and had a daughter together named Alana. How sweet her life would be if it were true.

"Walk out to me and I'll take your hand, then I'm going to help you lean back until your feet come off the ground."

They locked gazes again, and he whispered, "Don't worry. I'll hold you."

Her voice came out in the same whisper. "As you always have." Tears threatened to drench her cheeks, but she held them inside, taking her time with each step until she reached him. This lesson was too important to ignore.

"Have fun!" Dyna called, letting her know that Derric was out and dressed. Tamsin's hand was intertwined with Thane's, but she broke away to turn and lean into his arms.

"Now trust me and tip your head so your hair goes all the way into the water, then kick your feet up enough for me to catch you."

She tried twice but failed.

Thane said, "Let's take a break from this. Just

enjoy the water with me. Bounce in it, walk, swing your arms, whatever you wish to do."

"All right. I am more comfortable in it now, and it is much warmer to me." She spun around and nearly fell, but Thane caught her. She giggled as her feet found the bottom of the loch again, but she had a sudden urge to ask him a personal question. "Thane, are you married?"

He appeared surprised by her question, but he replied quickly. "Nay. I'm not married. I have no plans to marry."

"Why not?" She could respect that in a person, but she had to wonder why a man would say so. They seemed to get the most advantages from the relationship. A child, someone to clean their clothes, cook, take care of the home while the man hunted and provided for his family. It was the way of the world, apparently, so she thought every man would wish to be married. Didn't every man wish for a son or two?

Thane sighed and stared up at the clouds before he looked at her again. "I don't mind sharing with you, Tamsin. Mostly because I've not found anyone I would be interested in marrying. My brother and sister urge me to marry, but I'm not interested yet."

She tipped her head and asked, "Truly not interested at all?"

"There's something you don't know about me. My mother was not a kind woman. She raised Brian, Mora, and me with a rough hand. When Mora was but seven winters old, our mother dropped us off on the beach, threw a bag of clothes at us, and never returned."

Tamsin gasped. She couldn't imagine treating children so horrifically. "And you were but a few years older then."

"Four years. Brian is two years younger than me and Mora four. We had to find a cave to live in and foraged for our food. It was a most difficult life, but it was better than living with our mother. Her cruelty was too much. While we did go hungry on some days, we were never mistreated again, so we accepted it. We met a few others, and with them, found the castle that had been destroyed by fire and rebuilt what we could. It took us a long time, but I'm proud of what we've accomplished."

"But how does that affect your desire to marry?"

"Because I don't ever wish to watch a woman mistreat my bairns. If that is the way most marriages exist, then I don't want any part of it. I'll stay single. I cannot tolerate watching bairns mistreated."

Tamsin had never been more profoundly affected by anyone's words. She wished to hold Thane, hug him tight, and tell him all would be well if he married. She had to believe that things would be different. But would they?

Had it been different for her mother? Her past had not given her any better images of married life than his. "I'm sorry you've had such a terrible past. And it is even more difficult because of your siblings. My past is not much better. My mother died when I was young. My father promised me to Raghnall and I've never seen him or my sister again. But don't you feel differently now that you've been at Clan Grantham? When I watch Dyna and Derric with their bairns, it makes me hope for a better life. Is it not possible?"

Thane sighed. "I understand exactly what you are saying, and I will admit that observing everything and everyone at Clan Grantham gives me hope. I'm not sure if we are hoping for the same things, but hope is a blessing."

She nodded, wondering what he hoped for, but she didn't know him well enough to pursue that type of personal question. "I think Mora was verra happy here. It was good for her. She is a sweet lass, and you have done a fine job raising your siblings."

"Many thanks, and you are correct that being around other lasses was wonderful for her, but I've told you enough about my life. Come. Are you willing to try my suggestions again? Once you learn to swim, I promise that you will love it."

She smiled and arranged herself the way he'd guided her before. It took her three tries before she was able to do what he asked, but it finally happened.

"Tip your head back and look at the sky, not at me. The farther your head is back, the better you will do."

She did as he suggested, and to her surprise, he let go of her legs and she stayed up, filled with the exhilaration of floating on her own. She wished to squeal, her excitement nearly overtaking her, but then she lost it, and her head fell underwater.

"Hold your breath. I have you." Thane caught her, helping her to stand upright.

Her head broke through the water, and she burst into giggles. "I did it! May I try again? Please?"

The lesson continued, and the more time she spent with the man, the more she began to understand a concept that was totally new to her.

It was something that filled her heart with an odd joy, that made her want to be closer to him, that made her giggle like a wee lassie. Something totally different from anything she'd ever experienced, and she liked it.

She was falling in love with Thane MacQuarie.

CHAPTER THIRTY-TWO

MacDougall

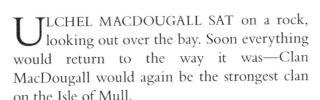

ULCHEL MACDOUGALL SAT on a rock, looking out over the bay. Soon everything would return to the way it was—Clan MacDougall would again be the strongest clan on the Isle of Mull.

He didn't care about the fool Robert the Bruce. He didn't consider the man to be the king of anything except perhaps the king of arseholes.

Once he accomplished his objectives, he'd be welcomed back into the clan as the brother to the chieftain instead of being banned because he'd hurt a lass.

The bitch had deserved it, but that was another tale for another day.

First, he had to regain his standing in his clan. Without his brother, he had no clan, no coin, and no bedchamber. He couldn't abide any of it.

Of course, MacClane had called him a fool for thinking he could take Duart Castle back from the Grants and Ramsays who held it now. Ulchel was smarter than anyone gave him credit for.

He knew the Ramsays could beckon a huge number of guards to take him out.

He knew the Grants had twice their number, as they were known as the strongest clan in the Highlands.

He knew the Ramsay women were archers who could shoot a man's bollocks off, if they wished to.

He wasn't foolish enough to go against either Clan Ramsay or Clan Grant.

But he'd been planning this for a while.

He'd paid men to attack Clan MacQuarie so they would wonder what was coming next. Told them to grab the faery if they saw her. Then he'd started rumors about attacking the clan and taking it over. He didn't care about MacQuarie Castle at all.

Not yet.

But he did need to halve the forces of Duart Castle, which would happen if they went to assist Chief MacQuarie. That was already set up. The rumor had wings already. He knew that would happen as soon as he had told Neal MacClane of his plans. And Neal had believed every word Ulchel had said.

The plan was in place. The Ramsays would hear that Clan MacQuarie was about to be attacked. They would send half their forces to aid MacQuarie, leaving Duart vulnerable.

His brother would be so proud of him.

But even his brother wouldn't know what else Ulchel had done. He'd seen Logan Ramsay and followed him one night. That was when he learned of the faery, the one who could grant wishes, but he also learned something else. This was information that would help his brother to get back in good standing with King Robert.

He'd witnessed the fool who had told Logan he was going to take over the isle. Once Ulchel had Duart Castle back for his clan, he'd send a messenger to the Bruce to tell him who was stealing cattle, lying, and doing his best to cause trouble on the Isle of Mull. He knew the identity of the man who vowed to control the isle.

No one else knew but Logan Ramsay. And he'd have to get rid of him somewhere along the way, but not yet.

The first step was capturing Duart Castle.

By the morrow, there would be a large group leaving Duart Castle for the western part of the isle. That would give him the time he needed.

Once they left, he would move in. Start a fire in front of the castle to draw the others out, then he could use the back entrance. If he were to guess, the Ramsays hadn't discovered the secret entrance his grandfather had made. He'd have a boat waiting not far away, and once he got the girl, he'd leave.

The girl would be his answer to everything. The faery had to grant him one wish, and he'd take back Duart Castle for Clan MacDougall. For his brother.

The morrow would be his day. They'd all see, and they'd sing his praises soon enough.

Duart Castle would be a MacDougall castle once again.

CHAPTER THIRTY-THREE

Thane

THANE DID HIS best to stay hidden as he approached Tamsin from behind. He'd learned she was practicing archery, but he wished to see how she was doing without alerting her to his presence. He didn't wish to intimidate her, and he feared if she saw him, she would freeze.

The truth of it was that he was jealous. This was a skill he needed, and he planned to learn to shoot in the future, even train some of his men to be archers. Their benefit from the top of a curtain wall is unparalleled.

Leaning up against a tree, he waited, surprised to see her fire two arrows in quick succession, one missing the target but the second one finding its mark just off the center.

"Spit and slime, I thought the first one was perfect."

He nearly chuckled but contained it. Eli had trained her apparently, not Dyna, because that was one of Eli's favorite expressions. Tamsin had chosen a most admirable woman to look up to.

Then he found himself doing something he hadn't expected. While she aimed the next arrow, Thane's gaze dropped to her curvaceous bottom, noticing the sweet globes peeking out from beneath her tunic. Tamsin was a beautiful woman, but she'd been in such unusual conditions that he'd not taken notice of her luscious curves. He surely did now.

Garvie was a fool. Thane's mind drifted to dangerous thoughts, but he decided to see where they took him. What if her husband didn't exist? Would Thane be drawn by Tamsin? He'd vowed to stay away from women, to stay far away from the call of any siren, though he would be embarrassed to tell anyone the reason why.

He'd hated his mother with such a passion that he swore never to love a woman, never to marry, never to have children.

Other thoughts had convinced him it was the most practical approach to his life, because he couldn't bear the other possibility happening.

He'd never implant a woman with his seed for the fear of finding her carrying his child. If he had to watch a woman raise his child the way he and his siblings were raised, he'd turn mad. To guarantee that this wouldn't happen, on the rare occasion when he'd had the need for release, he had pulled out before releasing his seed. While it had enraged one lass to see his seed on her leg instead of where it belonged, he vowed not to change. And he'd never had relations with that girl again since her actions had proven she only had one intention—trapping him into marriage.

That would never be his fate.

But watching Dyna and Derric had made him see a different side of life, something he'd never considered. They had a loving relationship and treated their bairns kindly. Not only did they treat them kindly, but they also spent time teaching them skills. All three could already fire arrows with their imitation bows. They carried themselves like miniature warriors, each one copying their mother.

He wondered if it was like that throughout their clan or if their relationship was an anomaly.

Watching the couple had also given him the unusual urge to wonder what it would be like to have true feelings for another. Curiosity made him want to explore such possibilities, to examine exactly what made the marriage happy. What the hell was this love the serving lasses all spoke of? He thought it to be something that existed only with the faeries, but Duart Castle had taught him otherwise.

He also had a niggling feeling, memories of another couple who had been happy, a vision from long ago, when he'd been very young, and Mora was just an infant. He had to guess it was his father. Had his mother been happy when their father was with them? He didn't have memories of the two together, for some odd reason.

He wanted answers to these questions but had no idea how to get them. His mother, if he ever did find her again, would not be free with this information. Of that much he was certain.

And watching Alaric and Eli carry on the way

they did, so open about their intimacies, made him think of strange possibilities. Had one lass he'd rescued changed the caveats he'd held on to for so long? Had Tamsin transformed him? Or was the hatred for his mother embedded so deeply that he would never be able to adjust?

Could he ever marry?

Not yet. He wouldn't do that to another until he gained the one thing that possessed his entire being, caused him sleepless nights, made him tense when certain thoughts entered his mind.

Vengeance. He needed vengeance for the wrong done to him, to Brian, and most of all to Mora. But first he had to locate the bitch who had done them wrong. His goal was to start searching the outer islands once he had thirty men. Then he would be confident that he could leave men behind to protect his castle while he and another group traveled to Coll and Tiree. She had to be on one of those islands.

Tamsin shot another arrow and hit her target nearly in the center. Thane applauded. He couldn't hold back any longer. "Tamsin, what a fine archer you have become. You must spend a considerable amount of time here."

She whirled, blushing and hiding her bow briefly before bringing it forward. Thane approached her and took her other hand in his. "I would never ask you to hide such a skill. Be proud of your work and all you've accomplished." He stared at her, the blush in her cheeks matching the pink of her lips, and he was powerless to stop what he did.

He bent down and kissed her, a brief kiss, and he had no regrets, married or not, because she tasted as sweet as he'd guessed she would. But the best part was she didn't push him away.

"Forgive me. I know you are married, but I couldn't stop myself." He cupped her cheek and then brushed a stray hair back.

"Not in my heart. I've never been married to him in my heart. My soul cries for another life, one with my daughter, but not my husband. Perhaps that is wrong, but it is how I feel. I just have to find a way to locate my daughter and bring her somewhere with me."

"If you find someone willing to go for you, I will gladly join in that effort. I hope you will not return to him alone, because I'm sure it would be a death sentence for you. Next time he won't try leaving you in the sea. He'll do worse, Tamsin. Please act with care."

"I will. I've spoken with Maitland and Eli about accomplishing what I said, getting Alana away from him. They said we would be welcome to live here at Clan Grantham."

"And you would both be welcome at Clan MacQuarie."

An excited voice interrupted them. "I'm coming too! I'm going to show you how well I can shoot, Thane. Wait until you see how good I am!" Magni flew onto the field, a bow and arrow with him, his sister strolling along behind him. "Lia is going to watch."

Lia approached them, her hands behind her back, while Magni settled his things. The lass looked exactly like what Thane's vision of an angel in heaven would look like. "I like to give Magni pointers, if I am able." Her smile was as sweet as her nature. "I pay close attention to all his lessons."

Tamsin asked, "Lia, your gown is lovely. Is it new?"

She wore a green gown, the color of a summer forest, with golden ribbons across the bodice. "Sylvi gave this to me. She said she hates it, so I was pleased to find that it fits me perfectly. And Lady Dyna said to consider it a gift. I do feel that way about it because it is light enough for a lovely summer day."

Magni said, "Thane. Watch this!" And he fired two arrows that both missed. "Awww …" He ran after his arrows, returning to try again. "Now I'm ready. Watch me."

Lia said, "Remember to take your time, Magni. You do much better when you take things slowly. And please do relax your shoulders."

Thane glanced over at Tamsin to see if she had any thoughts about the two. Every time he listened to Lia, it was as if an eighty-summers-old wise woman spoke from inside her. So wise and careful for a five-year-old, he often held his tongue because he was fascinated watching her.

There was something different about Lia.

"I'm going to find Alaric and chat with him. We will probably take our leave on the morrow. I'm glad to see you have healed quickly, Tamsin. If I can help at all, please ask."

Dyna joined them with her three bairns. "I'll

help Magni. You go do what you must, Thane. I hear you may take your leave soon."

"I may. On my next visit, may I reserve time to take archery lessons? I've always wished to learn."

"Of course! I'd be delighted to teach you. It will be interesting to see if you learn as quickly as Tamsin has."

He laughed and replied, "I doubt it."

Dyna's next comment surprised him. "Tamsin, are you returning to MacQuarie Castle or staying here?"

Tamsin looked up at Thane and asked, "Would I be able to return to your castle with you, Thane? I'd like to determine whether I can locate my daughter."

Thane paused for a moment, her request possibly forcing him to break one of his mantras. His one requirement of all his guards was that no adult females were allowed to live inside the castle walls. He couldn't risk watching any harsh treatment of a bairn. If he allowed Tamsin, he'd have to allow others inside.

But he had no choice.

"Of course."

What the in thunder was he to do now?

CHAPTER THIRTY-FOUR

Lennox

"WHAT THE HELL is going on?" Lennox MacVey asked as he approached his friend near the stables.

Sloan Rankin nodded his head toward the keep. "We need to talk. Hear the man out, then we can talk privately."

Lennox nodded, then led the way into his keep, heading toward the solar. He nodded to his mother to let her know to send a light repast in, then to join them. She knew everything that happened between his father and the other chieftains of the region, so Lennox considered her input invaluable.

His father had made her listen quietly in the background of all meetings, only offering her opinion when they were alone. She did the same for her son, and Lennox approved. But then again, his mother was quicker than any other woman he'd ever met.

Perhaps that was why he'd never married. He wanted an intelligent wife, but hadn't found one worth pursuing yet, ignoring his mother's persistent cajoling.

He opened the door to his solar, taking the seat behind the desk while Sloan and the third man took two seats on the opposite side.

Lennox started, "What has the two of you riled? Summer is here and the weather is lovely. Enjoy it."

Sloan's consternation was more than evident on his face; it was also in the sweat of his palms. Lennox couldn't help but wonder what had his friend so upset.

His mother had obviously picked up the same because she entered, a serving lass behind her carrying a tray with ale tankards along with a platter of berries and cheese. The serving lass settled everything and left as quickly as she'd entered.

His mother nodded to the two men, then took a seat against the back wall.

"Rut, feel free to sit closer," Sloan said. "We know you'll take everything in."

"I'm fine here, Rankin. Continue, Lennox."

Lennox didn't try to hide the glitter in his eyes at his mother's raised chin and narrowed eyes. The woman knew exactly how to handle herself and everyone else. He'd learned much from her over the years.

Lennox looked directly at Neil MacClane and asked, "What news have you for us?"

"MacDougall's brother is still here. Gone daft."

This was news, something that completely surprised him. He arched a brow, saying nothing, knowing MacClane would continue if he didn't speak. Rankin caught his gaze but kept his thoughts to himself.

"I saw him myself. Ulchel, the fool. He's gone daft. We have to stop him."

"Why?" Lennox asked, steepling his fingers in front of him as he leaned back in his chair.

"Because he's planning to attack Duart Castle. Then he's going after MacQuarie Castle. He told me. The fool has lost his mind. His brother kicked him out for attacking a lass in the clan. Now he'll do anything to gain his brother's approval. He wants back in the clan, and he believes that if he gets Duart Castle back, his brother will forgive him. That's his first step. After, he thinks he's going to control the isle by himself. Or rather, he plans to get Duart back for his brother, then he'll take over the rest of the isle."

They both smiled, Lennox hiding his better than Sloan.

"Aye, you two included. He thinks he'll have his brother's guards behind him and MacQuarie's men, then you two are next." Neil wiped the sweat from his brow before taking two long swigs of his ale.

Sloan snorted. "No one has enough soldiers to oversee the island. Only King Robert could drum up that many men. No one on the isle is large enough. Together, we don't have enough men to take over all the clans."

"I told you he was daft, did I not?" MacClane gave him an exasperated look that nearly made

Lennox smile. But there was more to this story. They all knew that MacDougall could attempt to seize control of the clans, but without the necessary number of trained guards, it was impossible. But any attack could still cost each of them some men. "Lennox, what the hell are we going to do?"

"Neil, MacDougall doesn't have enough men to conquer Duart Castle, much less MacQuarie Castle."

His mother stood, something unusual. "There is something else. Everyone knows that King Robert instructed the Ramsays to assume control of Duart Castle. There are two leaders of their guards—one is a Grant and the other a Ramsay. The Grants have a thousand men and the Ramsays another five hundred, which is why King Robert called on them. It would be a death sentence to strive to capture Duart Castle. There is more to this, and I wish to know what it is."

Lennox, surprised to see his mother participate, knew that she was as concerned as MacClane. Why, however, was his current question. What had triggered his mother to do the unthinkable and speak her mind in a chieftains' meeting?

The door opened with a bang, and a large man filled the doorway, his gray hair tied back with a leather thong.

Lennox nearly stood but stayed in his seat because his mother greeted the intruder before he could get his feet on the ground. She crossed her arms and nodded to the man. "Logan Ramsay. What the hell brings you here?"

"We have a problem, Rut. MacDougall plans to take over the isle, but in a way no one will suspect. And he's going after MacQuarie first."

CHAPTER THIRTY-FIVE

Tamsin

TAMSIN HAD TO admit that the sweet kiss she'd shared with Thane had set her heart soaring in a manner she'd never felt before.

She sat at a trestle table in the great hall, the group just finishing their meal made by the new cook they hired, and it had been wonderful. Tamsin had helped the lass add some spices and made a fruit tart on her own, and the group had enjoyed the sweet treat immensely.

It was time to move on.

After they finished and the bairns moved to their play area, Maitland said, "You are heading home on the morrow, Thane. How can we be of assistance to you? Oh, and bring your mare along on the next trip. I think the stallions will be settled by then." He chuckled at the expression of gratitude on Thane's face.

Thane said, "Much appreciation for that, Maitland. And I will bring a mare or two next time. I'll allow you to choose which will be the lucky one."

Dyna said, "Midnight Moon will choose. Don't worry. We've already had to pull Golden Gwyn away from him. He's getting randy."

Eli turned to Tamsin, bringing all the eyes to her. "What are your plans, Tamsin? I know you would like to gain your daughter back. How do you propose to do that? Have you some ideas?"

She didn't speak the words that popped into her mind—multiple choices.

I'll swim to her.

I'll hire someone. Whatever it takes.

I'll stick a dagger in my husband's eye, then kick him in the bollocks.

"I was going to ask if you had suggestions. As far as the law goes, since he tried to kill me twice, would I be able to walk away from the marriage? It would seem only right."

Maitland said, "Law goes with the husband, I'm afraid. If he wished to claim you again, he can. Mayhap I could speak with him, or Thane could approach him and see which way the bully is leaning. Thane's conversation could carry more weight, since he was a witness to both events. Your thoughts, Thane?"

Magni raced over into the middle of the group and said, "I forgot to tell you all something." The look on his face made Tamsin wish to hug him and tell him everything would be all right. It was fear unlike any she'd witnessed before.

Magni had everyone's attention, so he began his tale, "When I...I mean, when we got away from Garvie the first time, we got on a boat and hid in the forest. Lia's dress was green so we could hide really well, but while we were there, we saw two men talking …" The lad stopped to take a breath before he could continue.

"I saw two men, and they were talking about how they were going to take over the isle. That they wished to kill all the chieftains. They're traitors, are they not, Thane? Could you not hang them for trying to plan something like that?"

"Aye, they would be traitors to their country because King Robert sent us here in his name. Tell us exactly what you heard, lad," Maitland said, standing and taking two steps closer to Magni.

Alaric leaned forward, squeezing Eli's hand, just as the door banged open, making them all jump.

Magni took one look at the intruder and screamed, "That's him! That's the traitor!"

CHAPTER THIRTY-SIX

Logan

LOGAN CLOSED THE door, a grin on his face. "Good work, laddie. You have a fine memory, but I'm no traitor. I'm her grandfather." He pointed to Eli as he made his way into the middle of the group. "And I'm afraid I know most of these people."

People he'd missed desperately.

He'd have to listen to all their anger and their accusations, but he did what he'd had to do—take care of his Gwynie.

He couldn't live without her. It was that simple.

"Logan," Maitland called out, making his way over to him to clasp his shoulder before giving him a big bear hug.

"That's enough hugging and all that. I know you all missed me, but the lad's right. I have news to give you, so we can celebrate at a later date."

Magni moved in front of him and stared up the rugged man. "You are Logan Ramsay?"

"Aye, laddie. Why do you ask?"

"Because you're supposed to be mean. And you're smiling now. And isn't your wife the archer? Did you not train the best archers in all the land?"

Logan chuckled, loving all the stories and how they'd exploded, completely beyond the truth, but that was how legends were made, and even if he were being modest, he and Gwynie *were* legends.

He clasped the lad's shoulder and said, "Come. Sit down because I have to tell the adults what I've learned. Especially him." He strode over to Thane and shook his hand. "Logan Ramsay, MacQuarie. Pleased to make your acquaintance. There are men who plan to attack your castle at nightfall tomorrow."

"What?" Thane asked, standing to face Logan but not moving.

"What the hell, Logan?" Dyna barked at him. "That's a hell of an entrance."

Now that he had their attention, and they'd all shut their mouths about missing each other and all that nonsense, he grabbed a goblet of ale and a meat pie from a platter still on the table and sat down. Logan took one bite and said, "Let me know when you're all ready, and I'll tell you what I've learned."

He waited for everyone to settle, but one stopped him. He set his food down, looking up at the lass who stood in front of him, legs braced apart, arms crossed in front, gaze narrowed. "You want something, Elisant?"

She nudged his boot. "I'm waiting for my

apology for lying about where you were going. For not attending our wedding."

"We were there, and you know it."

"Still waiting." Her pursed lips told him she had a wee bit of Gwyneth Cunningham in her. He'd seen that exact look on his wife's face many times over the years.

"You can save all that for your grandmother."

Alaric stepped behind his wife, took her shoulders, and ushered her to a seat. "He has something important to tell us, so let's save this for later, wife. I'm all for tying him up until he apologizes, but there might be more at stake right now. Thane wants to hear the explanation."

"Glad to see someone can control her, Grant," Logan said and rolled his eyes.

"Grandfather!"

If he kept it up, he knew there was a distinct possibility he'd find an arrow aimed at his bollocks, so he decided to stop teasing the lass. She was young and had all those emotions and feelings rolling around inside her. He hadn't groomed her to be tough enough yet.

"All right, Eli. Calm yourself, but I do have important news for all of you." He stood, pacing in front of the group. "Ulchel MacDougall hopes to take Duart Castle back for his brother. He was ostracized from his clan because he attacked a local lass, and he thinks if he takes the castle, his brother will allow him back in. But he also believes that if he takes over MacQuarie's land first, he will have those guards to help him take

Duart back, and then, with his brother's assistance, he'll take over the entire isle, as Magni said ..."

"How do you know my name?" Magni asked, staring up at him.

Logan gave him the most honest answer he could. "Because I know everything about Scotland, lad."

Thane said, "Magni, please go sit with your sister."

"I'd like to meet the lass, Magni."

Magni led him over to her and said, "This is my sister, Lia."

"She's not your sister, but it is lovely to meet you, Lia." He took a moment to assess the lass carefully. He wasn't yet ready to admit to the others exactly what he'd learned about her, but he did wish to take in her presence himself.

"She is too my sister."

"Och, my mistake, lad. Of course she is." He ruffled Magni's messy hair. The lass looked to be five or six but had a presence of a hundred more years.

"Have you a wish, my lord Ramsay?" she asked, her fingers fanning the skirt of her green gown.

"That's the same green color my wife prefers for her leggings. It's the exact color of a forest in spring."

"It is my preferred color too. Dyna and Sylvi were kind enough to allow me to wear Sylvi's gown since she prefers leggings. When Magni and I ran away, I had no clothing but what I was wearing, and after living with the Garvies, well...it was not fit to wear again. The Corbetts graciously shared their clothing with both of us. This is my favorite gown. Your wish?"

He narrowed his gaze at her because he couldn't quite figure out the lass, and there'd been less than five people in his life who he couldn't assess instantly.

But she was different.

"No wishes. I'm a happy man, Lia. Take care of Magni."

Magni shouted, "But I take care of her. It's my job."

Logan patted the boy's head and said, "Of course you do. My mistake."

Thane asked, "With all due respect, could we return to the details of the attack on my castle, if you please?"

"Of course," Logan said, taking a seat again. "MacDougall has about a score of men he's hired with the coin his brother gave him before he banished him from Clan MacDougall. They are poorly trained, have paltry weapons, and only exist for coin. Most are English."

"Say no more," Maitland said with a snort.

"On the morrow?" Thane persisted.

"The plan is to attack during the evening meal."

"Then I guess we'll be leaving." Thane looked to Maitland to see if he had any suggestions.

Maitland said, "Alaric and Eli will go with you. Dyna, Derric, and I will stay here. What about the bairns?"

Magni shouted, "I'm going with Thane."

Thane said, "Nay, Magni. I'm going to leave you

and Lia here. I cannot worry about you during an attack. And I wish to help Tamsin too."

Maitland said, "I would recommend leaving just before dawn. You'll be home near high sun to ready your men. Traveling with a woman at night would not be advisable."

Logan added, "Leave the bairns here. You can retrieve them later. This castle has a thicker curtain wall."

Alaric looked at his wife and asked, "Are you ready for another battle, Eli?"

"I'll sit on the curtain wall with my bow aimed right at the ugly troll's chest."

Logan said, "Gwynie and I will stay here. I'll bring her at first light. I'll take my leave now. We'll be early enough for porridge, Granddaughter. Be prepared. Gwynie will be hungry."

He headed for the door, and just before he was ready to leave, Eli appeared next to him, her hand holding the door open.

"And Grandsire, there's a new rule in this castle. No banging the doors. I wish to keep our new place in good condition. Have you never seen the dent in the wall in the Ramsay great hall?"

Logan snorted and glanced over at his granddaughter with a smirk. "The wall is made of stone."

She arched a brow and glared at him.

She couldn't be serious, could she? Logan leaned over and planted a kiss on her forehead.

"I mean it, Grandpapa. I love you dearly, but no more door-slamming."

Hellfire, but he was proud of the lass. She was as bullheaded as he was. Gavin and Merewen had raised her right.

He grinned and only had one thought.

He couldn't wait to tell Gwynie.

CHAPTER THIRTY-SEVEN

Tamsin

———✦———

TAMSIN'S STOMACH ROILED as much as the landscape did as they approached MacQuarie Castle. It brought her back to the truth of what she had to deal with—that her daughter was being kept from her.

Walking into the Garvie manor home and demanding her daughter would only serve to get her locked in her chamber until Raghnall came to give her whatever punishment he considered appropriate for her transgression.

Refusing access to her child was a way for him to control her completely because he knew that Tamsin would never risk any harm coming to their daughter.

She had to find a way to steal her away from Raghnall. He had no interest in Alana and tried to kill Tamsin twice, so that was reason enough to steal her daughter away. If he knew of her crime, he would send the sheriff after her, but if he never knew what happened to Alana, he could hardly blame her.

If she were to guess, Raghnall probably believed Tamsin was dead. He'd left her to die.

She had to find a way to sneak in.

But first, they had to defend MacQuarie Castle from the attackers. She understood that.

As soon as the castle came into view, she glanced beyond it at the sea, the water not sparkling because of the clouds, the waves looking turbulent. It was a little rougher this day and she shivered, grateful this wasn't the day she'd been left to die. The waves would have been strong enough to push her under.

Alaric said, "Thane, go ready your men. You have a boat we can use to cross Loch Tuath? We will hide the boat and see what we can learn of Garvie's holding on the isle."

Eli added, "I'd love to see the area first. Great idea."

Thane nodded. "I'll have Artan take you over. He can show you what we learned. Before you go, Tamsin can add anything she would like you to check. I have no idea what buildings there are behind the gate, so she can fill you in with that information."

"I can draw a map for you in the sand. I think I know where the bairns are kept, but I'm not sure. I can go with you."

Alaric shook his head. "Nay, we do not wish to draw any attention, and I'm betting everyone on the isle knows who you are."

She blushed. "They do. You are right."

"Allow us a few hours to check out the

landscape of the isle so we can make a plan for the morrow after we rid Thane of MacDougall's men."

That made sense to her. Actually, it pleased her because she wasn't ready to face Raghnall quite yet.

When they approached from the front of the castle, Artan led Alaric and Eli down to the water while Thane led Tamsin and his two guards through the small village in front. He'd left Brian at home with Mora.

It wasn't long before many came out to stare at Tamsin.

And the eyes were not kind. She snuck a peek at Thane to see if he'd noticed the glares, but he kept his eyes locked on the gates, crossing the bridge and leaving the village behind. Relieved to have the curious looks of the local women behind her, she kept her horse behind Thane the best she could because it comforted her to have him nearby.

Once they approached, the gates were lifted promptly, but one guard called out to him, "We are admitting the lass, Chief?"

"Aye. Special circumstances is all you need to know."

She glanced at him after this conversation caught her. "You don't allow women inside your wall?" That couldn't be what they meant, was it?

"Aye, it's an old rule of mine. Since I hated my mother, the only female I allow inside the walls is Mora." He didn't say another word.

Tamsin had a sudden understanding as to why the women glared at her. She was getting special treatment.

Once inside, he said to Mora, "Please have Agnes ready a chamber for Tamsin. She'll be here for a few days."

"Gladly. Tamsin, is this the first time you've been here? How are things at Duart Castle? Isn't the weather looking stormy? Where are Magni and Lia?"

Tamsin took her time and answered all Mora's questions, following her up the stairs. They were inside the bedchamber with the door open when she heard someone enter the hall. Mora continued to ramble, but Tamsin was drawn by the sounds coming from below.

A guard she didn't know asked, "Chief, you are allowing women in the castle now? May I invite my wife inside?"

"Bearnard, these are special times. We have heard of an impending attack happening this eve, so please go fetch all the women and bairns and bring them inside the hall. We'll place pallets about, and they'll be sleeping here. Your wife can sleep in the same chamber as Artan's family. We have one large chamber above stairs with multiple beds. You and Artan may have it for your families. The rest can sleep on pallets here in the hall."

"Attack? By whom?"

"Invite everyone in, but please keep the reason quiet for now. Tell them we're feeding them this eve. We have the smoked venison, plenty for all, along with bread sent by the Granthams. Once you've accomplished that, I'll explain the rest. I'm going to speak with our men on the wall."

"Aye, Chief."

Tamsin had a sudden inspiration. "Do you have a back staircase in case of an attack, Mora?"

"Aye, at the end of the hall. It will take you to the rear wall where the door to the outside is. I'm hoping they'll never get inside. Do you think they will? Did none of the Ramsays come along to help? How many are attacking? Exactly when?"

Tamsin did her best to answer Mora's questions, but she had to admit that she was preoccupied. She was not going to wait inside the great hall for all those women of the village to find their way in to glare at her.

She'd be leaving by the back gate. There was no reason to risk anyone else's life. As soon as Eli returned and told her what building her daughter was in, she'd make her escape and go after Alana herself.

She would save her daughter, even if Tamsin lost her life in the pursuit.

CHAPTER THIRTY-EIGHT

Dyna

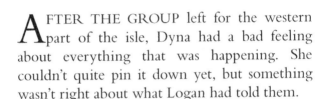

AFTER THE GROUP left for the western part of the isle, Dyna had a bad feeling about everything that was happening. She couldn't quite pin it down yet, but something wasn't right about what Logan had told them.

"I don't like this, Derric. Take the bairns inside. Have Astra take them to the cellars to play the hiding game. You know they love it. Take Magni and Lia too. Magni can help Astra with Sandor."

"Great idea, Diamond. Then I'll be back to help you."

Maitland headed toward the front gates, so Dyna caught up with him. "I have an odd feeling, but I can't define it yet."

"That's enough to get my attention. I'll talk with the guards, put them on alert."

"I'm going to walk around the wall as far as I can on the outside. Look for anything that has changed, any easy points to breach."

"Hold up, Dyna. Look who's coming up the path."

Logan and Gwyneth rode two horses abreast, Gwyneth waving to them. Dyna raced to their sides. "I'm so glad you're here, and I'm so pleased to see you, Gwyneth. I'd like to chat, but I'm having a bad feeling, so I'm going around the curtain wall. Derric took the bairns into the cellars."

"Say no more. We'll head inside and help in any way." Logan took the reins of his wife's horse to lead them to the stables. "I'm sensing things are not right. Could be the bastard used trickery to divide our forces."

"Dyna, do what you and Maitland must do. Do not worry about us." Then she turned to her husband. "Logan, we're going up on the wall," Gwyneth said, pointing to a spot. "Right there. I want that spot. Find me a stool."

They went their separate ways, and Dyna's unease grew. Something was about to happen, but what? She took the time to stroll around Duart Castle's curtain wall. It was her favorite walk because one could see water on three sides, almost. The Sound of Mull, the Firth of Lorne, and Loch Linnhe surrounded the coast. She'd even promised to one day take the bairns down on a stretch that looked quite serene.

Not today. She held her bow with such a tight grip that she knew she was missing something. Opening the back gate, she rounded the side of the keep just as the goat herder crossed the entrance to deliver the day's milk, but he headed toward the stable, not his usual path.

Perhaps he'd seen someone inside he wished to speak with.

The man disappeared, and within seconds, she caught the flash of fire when the back of the stable ignited.

"Maitland! The horses!"

She ran to the stone building, opening the side door and rushing in, opening up each stall and slapping the horses. Midnight Moon wouldn't move, so she tugged on him, finally getting him outside. He acted strange but there was no time to figure why the beast was fussing, just get him safe. Once he was out, a voice caught her.

"Diamond! She ran away! Catch her."

Tora was headed straight for her mother, way ahead of Derric, so Dyna waved him back inside. "I'll get her. Go back with the others, Derric. The attack has started."

Tora said, "I don't like that man, Mama." She pointed to the back of the stable. "He went in there. I save you."

A man charged out from behind the wooden building, the goat herder, and the worst happened. He headed straight for Tora, still a good distance away from her.

Dyna screamed, grabbing Tora before the man could get to her, but he lunged for Dyna instead. She tossed her daughter up on Midnight Moon's back and said, "Ride horsey out back, Tora. Go!"

Tora took the reins and to Dyna's utter surprise, the animal calmed right down. The man came straight for her, a sword in his hand.

An arrow sliced through the air over her

head and into the man's leg, but it didn't stop him. Midnight Moon changed his direction and danced behind them, and then did something that totally surprised Dyna. He reared, Tora hanging tightly to the reins as the beast came down on the man's back, knocking him to the ground at the same time that a second arrow hit him in the neck.

Maitland was behind her. "Get your daughter! I'll get the rest of the horses out."

Gwyneth yelled, "Get your daughter and get up here, Dyna. There are ten more men coming this way, and they don't look friendly!"

Maitland cursed, but the gates were already locked. Dyna took her daughter off Midnight, and she kissed him. "Many thanks, Moon boy."

"I ride horsey, Mama."

"You did, and you did a fine job hanging on. Now get your bow ready. We have men to stop." Tora's arrows wouldn't hurt anyone, but the lass didn't know that. Dyna raced up the stairs to the top of the wall, carrying Tora, then found a spot a distance away from Gwyneth, arranging herself, her daughter, and her arrows before firing.

Logan joined them, cursing, pulling his own bow out. "Bastards. The threat to MacQuarie was a diversion. I heard them planning to get the girl." He peeked over at Dyna. "What the hell do they want with Tora?"

"Was Tora the one they wanted? He was going to grab her, but one girl looks the same as the others next to strangers," she said. "Which one was he after? There are four here."

The answer came to them sooner than expected. Three men came close to the gates and said to the two guards there, "Give us the faerie, and we'll let you live."

They were all dead within seconds, enough arrows protruding from their bodies, but they weren't done yet. Broc came around the parapets, bellowing, "They're coming in the back entrance!" He raced down the staircase, his weapon readied.

Five men came around the side of the castle inside the wall, swords in hand. Maitland, Broc, and two other guards charged them. Broc took on two men, parrying and thrusting at both until he struck one in the leg, forcing him to the ground.

Maitland went after another man but chuckled. "You think to take me down with that paltry weapon?" The two fought while the two guards took on the remaining two invaders.

Clashing swords rent the air and arrows flew, but they weren't finding their target.

Dyna reached for Gwyneth, staying her hand. "You're getting too close to our men. I'll get them."

"Blasted eyes," Gwyneth cursed.

Logan said, "Mine are no better. I'm moving." He took off down the walk on the curtain wall to gain closer access. His first arrow struck the man one of the guards fought, catching him in the back and he yelled in pain, falling to the ground.

Broc took a wide swing and struck his opponent in the side, nearly slicing him in half. He was dead in seconds. Logan took another man out, then Maitland's attacker fell next by his sword.

Dyna and Gwyneth jumped when a lone invader come across the wall, landing in the walkway. Dyna shoved her daughter behind her, but she caught the man's excitement when his eyes found Tora. "Give me the lass!" he cried, running straight at them. They both fired at the same time, hitting him in two places. Tora called out, "I got him, Mama."

The battle was over.

Dyna hugged her daughter tight, then leaned back against the wall and said, "Nice shot, Gwyneth. I know it was yours that hit him in the leg."

"Damn eyes. I was aiming for his heart."

Dyna smiled and sat down, but said, "Doesn't matter. You got him." Then she thought of her daughter running to her, away from Derric, something unusual.

"Tora, why did you run outside?"

"I had to save you from the bad man."

"How did you know he was bad?"

She pointed to her forehead and said, "I saw him here."

Logan returned in time to overhear the conversation. "Does that mean she's the faerie?"

Dyna said, "There are four girls here. Astra, Sylvi, Tora, and Lia. I don't know which one is the faerie?"

Tora said, "I know, Mama." She glanced at her mother, a wide smile on her face.

Dyna, sitting a short distance away, whirled her head to look at her daughter. "Who is the faerie?"

Tora looked at her mother and smiled. "We all are. But I'm this kind." Tora pointed to her forehead again, then walked over to her mother, bent over to look in her mother's eyes, tipping her head upside down, and pointed to Dyna's forehead. "Just like you."

"The others are different."

CHAPTER THIRTY-NINE

Tamsin

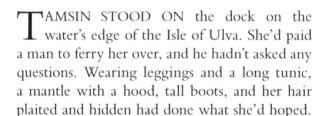

TAMSIN STOOD ON the dock on the water's edge of the Isle of Ulva. She'd paid a man to ferry her over, and he hadn't asked any questions. Wearing leggings and a long tunic, a mantle with a hood, tall boots, and her hair plaited and hidden had done what she'd hoped. It kept her from being recognized as Garvie's wife.

It was nearly dark and Raghnall would be half in his cups by now, his usual nightly activity, and that was just how she wished to find him. She thought about going after her daughter first, but she had unfinished business with her husband.

Risking imprisonment didn't worry her now that she knew she had friends who would stand by her. She could actually thank Raghnall for helping her get away from Ulva, and in doing so, she'd met wonderful, loving people, the kind of people one looked up to, who believed in helping others. Eli, Alaric, Dyna, Maitland, Derric, Magni, Astra… so many she'd met.

And then there was Thane. She didn't yet know what to make of him, because she was afraid to let him get too close. After all, her father had dumped her on another man for coin, and her husband had tried to kill her twice. How could she ever trust any man?

She knew it would be difficult to allow another man into her life, especially to trust one. But Thane had done one important thing for her—he'd given her hope. Hope that life could be something wonderful if one was surrounded by the right people.

They would have time to get to know each other better if she survived this venture. She would not leave the island alive without her daughter. This much she knew to be true.

Making her way past the empty market buildings, the busy tavern, the inn, and all the other establishments controlled by Raghnall Garvie, she took a deep breath and said a quick prayer. Striding up to the entrance, she paused for a moment to make sure her bow and arrow were well hidden under her mantle. Satisfied, she inhaled deeply and made her way up to the gates of hell.

Raghnall's land.

"I'd like to see my husband, please."

Odart came forward. "Lady Garvie? Is that truly you? But I thought…"

"I know you did. This is the second time I've escaped an attempt on my life by you and my husband. I've come to claim my daughter and

I'll take my leave, never to bother either of you again."

Odart's face gave away his thoughts, but she didn't care. He thought she'd never accomplish what she intended, but he was about to see a different Tamsin Garvie. "Please lead me to Raghnall, Odart."

"Of course, my lady."

The men they passed snickered, making odd comments about her clothing and other things she chose to ignore. They'd remember her name after this night. If she had learned anything from Dyna Grant and Elisant Ramsay, it was to have confidence in your abilities. Being a woman meant you were strong, not weak like her husband wished her to believe.

He would learn the truth.

They entered their manor home, moving to the back of the house, away from her old bedchamber. Odart knocked on a door to a chamber she'd never been in because it had always been locked. Raghnall bid him to enter, so he did, but Odart motioned for her to wait. Within a few moments, a young lass exited, tears on her face, a bruise already visible on one cheek. She ran, and Tamsin's heart went out to her. Then she heard a loud bellow.

She smiled because she recognized that bellow. Drunken Raghnall.

Odart stepped out and said, "Enter, Tamsin."

She stepped inside as Raghnall got out of bed and lit a candle, grabbing trews to don, which he did quickly. The room was twice the size of their bedchamber. Tamsin closed the door behind her, taking the key, and said, "I've come for Alana. Allow us to leave, and I'll never bother you again."

Raghnall laughed. "You stupid cow. The bitch who wouldn't die. Who keeps saving you? Tell me and I'll have his heart cut out."

"Where is Alana?"

"I'll never tell you. She's mine to do with as I wish. She'll service me well in a few years."

Tamsin's hands shook, the dampness settling in, something she had expected. And as soon as it started, she had vowed to act, or she would surely lose her advantage. The first step was to remove her mantle, which she did, dropping it to the floor.

Raghnall reached for his tunic and went to put it over his head, giving her a perfect target. Just as she'd practiced over and over again, she whipped out her bow, grabbed an arrow, aimed and fired, catching him exactly where she aimed.

She'd taken her husband completely by surprise.

The arrow embedded in the flesh of his groin, between his private parts and his leg. He bellowed, collapsed to the ground, landing hard, his tunic falling to the side.

She spun around and locked the door to keep Odart from entering, taking the key and putting it in her mantle that was now on the floor. Her husband lay there, his hands on the arrow, trying to pull it out, but he screamed as loud as a banshee.

"Husband, you scream like a lass."

"Take it out, Tamsin. You put it there. I'll have you hanged for this. Take the arrow out. I'm bleeding. There is blood all over my hands now." He slid himself closer to the bed, grabbing the covers to wipe the blood from his hands, but the wound continued to bleed. "Help me. I'm ordering you to remove this or I'll kill you, Tamsin."

She strode over and said, "You've already tried that twice. Now, where is Alana?"

"Dead. She's dead. I killed her."

She lost all sense of reason and did the unthinkable. Recalling Dyna's words, she kicked him in his bollocks. He grabbed his privates and turned his head, vomiting all over his legs.

An anger overtook her. She moved to kick him again, but he held his hands up and said, "Enough. She's alive."

"Where?"

He ground out, "You'll never find her."

"Where?" She placed her foot on his sac and pressed down.

Raghnall screamed and passed out.

Where the hell was Alana?

She had to be in one of the buildings. Taking the key out to open the door, she wasn't surprised to find Odart standing there, looking guilty.

Tamsin took a step back, allowing Odart to look in at Raghnall.

Odart paled and held his hands up. "I'll do whatever you wish, my lady."

"Take me to Alana."

CHAPTER FORTY

Thane

WHEN THANE LEARNED Tamsin was missing, it was as if someone had kicked him in the gut, then spun him around to do it again.

Mora had been undone, but he'd calmed her down. "It's not your fault, Mora."

Her breath hitching, she took his hand. "But I told her how to leave. I told her where the door was. And I told her about the back gate. And you'll hate me forever because she's the one for you, Thane. I'm sure of it. She's going to melt your heart and in a verra good way. She's going to make you understand that life is to be lived and not thrown away seeking vengeance for someone who doesn't matter. She's teaching you how to love."

Nothing anyone had ever said to him had hit him as hard as his sister's words. Because they were true. So true. Tamsin was changing him in so many ways that it scared the hell out of him.

He had to find her.

"Stay here, Mora. I'll take Alaric and Eli with me. Promise me you'll stay here, and I promise to bring her back."

She'd given him a swift hug and said nothing more, urging him down the staircase. Her lack of words spoke louder than her previous ones. She wanted this for him.

For them.

Her last words caught him just before the door closed. "We all need her, Thane. Find her and bring her home."

Home. Something he'd wished to make for his brother and sister, but he hadn't quite accomplished it yet. He'd been too busy focusing on revenge. Finding their mother to right her wrong.

Now he was headed, in the dark, across the water to the Isle of Ulva. "Do you have a suggestion, either of you, on how to proceed?"

Alaric said, "Eli and I will go in the largest building, you go in the next. There is no other way. There are only four buildings in use near his home. The main manor home and three behind it. I would guess Garvie would be in the largest one, so we'll go there. The lass is probably kept in one of the back buildings. One looked to be more in use than any other. We listened for bairns but didn't hear any."

Thane gave them a wry smile because he knew exactly why. "Magni said they were not allowed to speak. They had to sit quietly, or they'd be punished."

When they approached the dock, something

else occurred to him. "Did you know that we were treated the same? It's the reason why Mora will ask four or five things at once. She had to get everything out quickly because she'd be slapped and forced to hold it all in."

Eli clasped his shoulder and gave it a squeeze. "You have done a fine job with both of your siblings."

"It's why I let her ask as much as she needs to." He grinned and said, "When I told her where I was going, it was the first time she had little to say. Just told me to find Tamsin."

They reached the island and climbed out. Because it was dark, no one was around the pier, so they tied the boat and disembarked. It was a short walk to the open gate with no one around to protect it. The sounds of drunken revelry came from the tavern.

Alaric said, "Eli and I will take the main home. You start in the building behind it."

Thane nodded and headed toward the back of the building. Listening carefully, he was surprised to find there was no one about. Raucous voices carried from the inn closer to the water, but that was all.

As soon as he stepped behind the manor home, he saw a path that went on through the forest and between three buildings: two on one side and one on the other side of the path. The buildings were a bit behind where he stood, but beyond the path that headed into the forest, it was so dark he could make nothing out.

Voices cut through the night from the farthest

building, so he hurried to see if he could uncover who was inside. Moving closer, he waited.

One voice was Tamsin's, that much he recognized. But the other voice was vaguely familiar.

"Where is Alana? I want my daughter."

"You'll never get her. She belongs to Raghnall, not you. He'll do what he wishes with her."

"Where is she? Tell me now or you'll find an arrow embedded in your black heart!"

The woman laughed, and it sent a chill down his spine.

"You think you frighten me? You are nothing to me. Just someone to do my bidding …"

Thane bent over at the waist, holding his head, memories flooding through him that were so painful, he couldn't bear to listen anymore. Visions of a sobbing Mora, of Brian fighting the bitch, of himself as a young lad, screaming at his mother to stop …

His mother! This voice was his mother's voice! Could it be possible? She'd taken them across Loch Tuath and dumped them on Mull. Of course. Why had he thought Coll or Tiree? His thoughts tore in so many directions that he had trouble making sense of everything, but the woman continued to babble on. This was definitely the voice of his mother.

A figure came from behind the building, carrying a sleeping child of around two years old. Alana. It had to be Alana.

The figure headed straight for the forest. She was getting away with Alana, probably with the intent to hide the lass where no one would ever find her. In the forest of Ulva, one could probably hide for many moons.

First, he'd kill his mother, then he'd go after the woman carrying Tamsin's daughter. He had time.

Surely, he did. He'd settle the vengeance that had ripped at his soul for years. For the siblings who'd been deserted, left to fend for themselves in the middle of the wilderness with nothing but a few pieces of clothing. For the abuse, the cruelty, the neglect. He could gain the revenge he'd sought for so long. Finally, it was all within his reach!

A sudden shock hit him, a jolt as if a bolt of lightning tossed him into the air and flipped him onto his backside.

His gaze went to the path into the forest.

This was no longer about his mother.

This was about the child.

An innocent child who was being controlled by people who cared nothing about her. Who was completely at their mercy—to be beaten or starved or abused in any number of ways.

As much as he experienced the overpowering need and desire to rail against his mother, to stick a knife in her heart, he was drawn by the innocent lass being stolen away.

The child innocently tossed into the melee. Into the middle of a life of despair, of no direction, no hope. Of listless repetitions of devastation. Of slaps and lies and starvation. A wee Mora.

Tamsin had changed him.

Thane headed down the path toward the woman carrying the child.

Alana.

He was no longer seeking vengeance but love.

Tamsin had changed him in a way he hadn't thought possible.

Irrevocably different.

A vast improvement over the man who had diligently sought vengeance against the evil being who had ruined his life.

He followed the woman down the path deep into the forest where the trees were so thick, the moonlight did little to light his way. It didn't take long before he caught up with her. She wasn't a large woman, and she carried a sleeping child in her arms, slowing her down even more.

"Stop. If you hand her over, I won't kill you when I reach you."

To his surprise, the woman stopped and turned around, handing the child over immediately. "Please don't kill me. She made me do it."

"This is Alana, is it not?"

"Aye. Raghnall's child. I hate that woman. She forced me. Don't tell her I gave her up. Please. She'll have me whipped."

"Who? What's her name?"

"Dagga."

His knees nearly buckled at the name he'd wished to hear over the years, but he held strong, taking Alana into his arms, still asleep. Glancing down, he smiled because the wee lass looked exactly like her mother.

"Go home and never come back," he said to the woman, and she ran.

He cuddled Alana close to his chest to keep her warm, snuggling her the best he could as he turned around, heading back down the path. As soon as he broke out of the forest, Tamsin appeared, taking one look at him and crying out. "Alana? Is it Alana, Thane?"

He nodded. "I think so. She's beautiful and unhurt. She looks just like you, Tamsin."

Tamsin reached them, checking the soft cheeks of the sleeping bairn tucked against his chest before breaking into tears. "It's her. My sweet daughter." She threw her arms around them both, tears now covering her cheeks. "My thanks to you, Thane. I feared she was lost."

She kissed her daughter's forehead, and the lass opened her eyes and whispered, "Mama? I don't like Gwamama. Take me away."

Thane said, "Can you hold her, Tamsin? I have something else I need to tend to." Then he leaned over and kissed Tamsin's cheek.

"Come back? Please, Thane?" she asked when he slipped Alana into her arms.

"Oh, you have my promise on that. I wish to learn all there is to know about you, Tamsin Garvie."

Her eyes misted and she whispered, "You have no idea how happy that makes me."

Thane noticed a couple coming toward them. "Alaric, we have Alana. Will you watch over them? I have something to take care of."

"Absolutely. What is it? Can we help?"

"Nay, this is something I need to do alone. The woman who held Alana is my mother."

Tamsin gasped. "Are you Raghnall's brother?"

Thane shrugged. "I'll find out."

Then he strode toward the house where Dagga lived.

He whistled, a calmness settling over him unlike any feeling he'd ever had before.

He was going to visit his mother.

Vengeance would finally be his.

CHAPTER FORTY-ONE

Thane

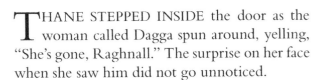

THANE STEPPED INSIDE the door as the woman called Dagga spun around, yelling, "She's gone, Raghnall." The surprise on her face when she saw him did not go unnoticed.

"Greetings, Mama."

"Thane! My dearest boy. Where have you been? You got lost in the forest, and I've been searching for you ever since. Where is Brian? Mora. Are they hale? My, but didn't you grow into a large man. You're taller than my Raghnall."

He leaned against the door to prevent her exit, crossing his arms as he took in the old cottage, not much different from how it'd been eight years ago. This was where they'd lived. Or rather been imprisoned. They'd never gone into the main house, only allowed out in the back to work. This had been his hell—The Isle of Ulva. She'd taken a boat over to the Isle of Mull and dropped them in the middle of the beach, probably hoping they would die from exposure.

"And why would you care if Mora and Brian were well? What if they were both dead? Would you care?"

"Of course I would. It wasn't my fault."

"The hell it wasn't. I remember it as clearly as if it were yesterday. I recall every word that came out of your lying mouth, Mother Dearest." He glanced over at the wall where the pegs for outerwear hung in the same place, a whip hanging from the middle peg.

He sidled over to the pegs, removed the whip, and his mother ran for the door. He reached out with one arm, and she tried to punch him, but he chuckled. "Not so fast. I'm not finished with you yet."

She cursed at him and punched him, but he lifted her easily and did the same thing to her that she used to do to Mora.

He hung her up on the peg by the back of her clothing. How he wished they were both here to watch their mother hanging in the air, all four extremities swinging with anger.

"Let me down. I'm an old woman. You can't treat me like this."

"I can and I will." He picked up the whip and snapped it against the floor.

"You wouldn't. Thane, I always loved you best."

"Who is my father?"

She snickered, so he cracked the whip again.

"I will use it if you don't give me the answers I am seeking. All I want from you is information." He thought for a moment. "Then I wish to never see you again. Gaol would be a fitting new home for you. But we're not ready for that yet. My father. Who is he?"

"You ignorant fool. Your parents are dead." She spit off to the side, far away from him. "Now let me down."

Oddly, this surprised him. He'd never considered the possibility that she wasn't his true mother. Why the hell had they been living with her all those years? And was Mora his true sister? Brian his brother? This brought up more questions than ever. "My parents? You're not my mother? Tell me more." Shocked by this possibility, he had to pursue the truth.

"Nay. I'm not your mother. You were all stolen away to sell to a man in Europe, but he changed his mind. So, I put you to work to make my hard life easier, but I tired of all three of you, especially that whiny sister of yours. No one else would buy the three of you because you were all so miserable, so I got rid of you."

"Did you consider the possibility that we were miserable because of the way you treated us?"

"I treated you fine. I fed you, didn't I?"

"Aye. Barely. Moldy bread and… Never mind. Where did you find us?"

"I don't know," she grumbled.

He cracked the whip. "Where?"

"Raghnall!" she called out. "Come save your mother!"

Eli entered and took the spot next to Thane. "Please. Allow me to stay," she whispered to him. "It would please me so much to assist you."

He gave Eli a slight nod before he repeated himself. "Where?"

"Raghnall?"

Eli smiled and stepped in front of her. "Your son is dead. Tamsin put an arrow in his bollocks, then kicked him there to uncover Alana's location. He removed the arrow and bled out within minutes, killing himself. He can't save you."

"Why, that little whore killed my son?"

Eli reacted so quickly that she startled Thane, slapping the woman hard across the face. "She is not a whore. Close your mouth or I will sew your lips shut with a needle and thread, you witchin' bitch."

Dagga's eyes widened, then she mumbled, "Coll. We stole you from Coll. All three of you. Raghnall killed your parents. It was a small village of five cottages."

Thane dropped the whip on the floor and said, "You can leave her there if you wish."

Alaric came in behind him and said, "I'll tie her up and take her to the sheriff on Mull."

Thane nodded, walking outside and straight into Tamsin's arms. He didn't know what to do, what to say. He just needed her. Alana slept on Tamsin's shoulder, and he leaned in, clutching the woman as if she were all he had. And he let out what had been building up inside him for years. The tears erupted and flowed so easily but he didn't care.

Tamsin did the one thing no one had ever done for him—she held him close.

And he cried. All the tears he'd kept inside for

so many years. He cried the tears for everything they'd endured. For wee Mora, for Brian, and for a little boy named Thane who'd been forced to grow up too quickly.

Tamsin whispered, "It's behind us now. All of it, Thane."

CHAPTER FORTY-TWO

Tamsin

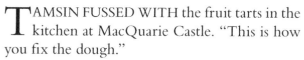

TAMSIN FUSSED WITH the fruit tarts in the kitchen at MacQuarie Castle. "This is how you fix the dough."

Mora played with the pastry while Alana and Lia watched. "How's this? I think I did it right. Does it look right? Should I pinch it more? Or less?"

Tamsin said to Mora, "You did a fine job. It is lovely and will taste even better."

Then she gave a wee cup of honey to Alana and said, "Sprinkle a wee bit across the top like this." And her daughter did exactly as she had done, giggling all the while she sprinkled. "I wuv you, Mama."

"I love you all," Tamsin said, offering the honey to Lia. "Would you like to try?"

"Nay, allow Alana to do it. She did such a fine job."

She washed her hands and helped her daughter to wash the honey from her fingers, though the child was busy licking them as fast as Tamsin could clean them.

When they finished, she handed a tray to Mora with a smile. No matter how Tamsin tried, she couldn't get the image out of her mind of Mora as a child being hung on the pegs by Dagga, scaring her with the whip. The sheriff of Argyll had arrested Dagga the next day and taken her away, her list of crimes so long, he left shaking his head while the woman cursed him out, declaring her innocence.

She helped Alana down off the stool and said, "Why don't you three take the desserts out to the sideboard and I'll clean up. We can eat once the pottage is done." The three took off giggling in unison, trying to decide which berry tart would taste the best.

Thane came in once the girls left, coming up behind her, wrapping his arms around her and kissing her neck. Tamsin giggled and wriggled away from him. "I'll be done soon."

He leaned against the table in the center while she finished. "Can I help at all?"

"Nay. All is well." She smiled at him and stood on tiptoes to give him a quick kiss, one he deepened, his tongue mating with hers briefly before she ended the kiss.

"You are such a good mother, Tamsin. You impress me with your patience every day."

"Many thanks. I hope to undo any damage done by that evil woman." She finished and set her linen cloth down to dry, then fell into his arms. "Thane, I've never been happier than I am at your home. My thanks for making us feel so welcome. I'm sorry I cannot go as quickly as you like in our relationship, but—"

He set a finger against her lips. "I am more than happy with our relationship the way it is. I swore never to allow a woman in my home, if you recall, so I've come a long way."

"And I swore to never marry again. And if I had the chance, I'd have told my sister Meg never to marry. Now I feel differently. I hope to find my way back to her someday." If she only had some idea exactly where they had lived, but she didn't. She'd never paid attention to such details since they rarely left their property.

"I'll help you when you are ready."

"I don't even know what isle we lived on, Thane. It will be quite a challenge. But I thank you for your patience, especially with our relations. I am quite naïve."

"I'm in no hurry. I'd prefer to take our time to make sure we are right for each other. We both had difficult times in our past. It's important we get past those times before we commit. That's my belief. I'll not rush you, lass."

She rested her head against his shoulder and said, "I agree." He rubbed slow circles across her back as he folded his arms around her.

She whispered, "But I do believe I'm falling in love with you, Thane. You've shown me a world I didn't know existed."

He kissed her forehead and said, "I love you

too, lass. You've brought me happiness I've never known." He cupped her cheeks and kissed her.

"One step at a time."

Thane bolted up in bed, nearly letting out a bellow, but stopping himself just before his mouth opened. He'd had the same nightmare again. His father pushing him toward his brother and telling him to go across to the forest.

He wiped the sweat from his face and closed his eyes, forcing himself to picture the woman in his dream. He needed to see her face so badly that he'd hoped to have this dream every night.

With the discovery of Dagga and her litany of lies had come another realization. Had he witnessed his parents' murder? If so, was it truly Raghnall who had killed them? But the more important piece of the puzzle that had emerged from Dagga's admission was the answer to the identity of the woman in his dream. It wasn't his aunt.

The woman in his dream was his mother.

Epilogue

Dyna

D YNA, MAITLAND, ALARIC, Eli, and Gwyneth sat around the hearth at Duart Castle. "Do you think they'll marry after all they've been through?" Dyna asked.

Maitland said, "I think Thane and Tamsin will be married within six moons. After the trauma each one has been through, they have to learn to trust again. Not an easy thing to do. Once that happens, they'll marry. The important piece is that I don't think Alana shows any negative effects from the evil woman who cared for her. She is a sweet little thing."

Gwyneth said, "Don't think it can't come out later in life, but I agree with you. I think Tamsin's goodness overpowered the bad in Alana's life."

The door banged open, and Eli hopped out of her seat. "Spit and slime, Grandsire! Stop. Banging. The. Door!"

Logan stepped inside, glared at his granddaughter, then stepped back out, closed the door, and opened it quietly. "Does this suit my bossy granddaughter?"

Eli laughed and said, "Aye, my thanks to you, Grandpapa. Now come inside and tell us what you've learned."

He came in with a sigh, moving over to take a chair next to his wife. "Gwynie, who raised our granddaughter to be so bossy and stubborn?"

Gwyneth rolled her eyes and ignored him.

Logan continued, "I didn't learn much—only one thing. Word was we brought a healer and faeries to Duart Castle. No names have been mentioned. But one of the faeries is supposed to grant wishes. A green faery."

Dyna sat forward, her eyes wide. "The green maiden?"

"Which one?" Eli asked. "Who is the green maiden? Is it Lia?"

Logan raised his arms in question. "What the hell is a green maiden? That is what I'd like to know."

Eli sat back, both hands cupping her cheeks. "Oh my."

"What is it?" Alaric asked.

"The green maiden. Doesn't she grant wishes? Something of that nature?"

"That could be, but I don't know why anyone would think we have a green faery," Logan said.

"But we might," Eli said quietly, looking from one face to the other to see if it had dawned on anyone else.

"What?" Gwyneth asked.

Eli looked to Dyna. "You heard her."

"What the hell, Eli? Out with it," Logan demanded.

Dyna said, "Calm down, Logan. When we first met Lia, she asked us if we had any wishes."

Eli bolted out of her chair and hopped in the same spot three times. "Oh…."

"What?" Alaric shouted, standing next to her.

"I told her I wished for my grandmother to come back to me. That I missed her so much. That I wanted both my grandparents here."

Logan snorted. "So, what does that mean?"

"You're both here. She granted my wish! Lia is the green maiden!"

Logan shook his head. "We were already here. You just hadn't caught us yet. That doesn't mean that Lia is the green faery, or maiden, or whatever. She didn't make us appear, Eli. But I do know one thing. Lia is not Magni's sister."

"How do you know that?" Eli asked.

"I can't say. But she's not. There's something different about the lass, and I believe she's the one they're after," Logan replied.

Gwyneth said, "We may never find out who or what she is, but I know one thing for certain."

"What?" Maitland asked.

"This isn't over."

THE END

www.keiramontclair.com

DEAR READER,
Thanks for picking up the first book in my new series!

I'm hoping to add another three books to the series. The next book will focus on Lennox MacVey. His heroine will be…You'll see! As in any of my series, you can expect to see much more of Thane, Tamsin, Magni, Lia, and all the members of Clan Grantham.

And Logan and Gwyneth.

The Scots love tales of faeries and magik, so I thought I would go back and dip into the paranormal aspect a wee bit. I hope you like it.

I'm enjoying the Isle of Mull. I hope you are too.

As always, this book is completely fictional. Please let me know what you think at *keiramontclair@gmail.com*.

Happy reading!

Keira Montclair

NOVELS BY
KEIRA MONTCLAIR

CLANS OF MULL
THE PLIGHT OF A SCOTTISH LASS

HIGHLAND HUNTERS
THE SCOT'S CONFLICT
THE SCOT'S TRAITOR
THE SCOT'S PROTECTOR
THE SCOT'S VOW
THE SCOT'S DESTINY
THE SCOT'S WARNING
THE SCOT'S RECKONING
THE SCOT'S LEGACY

HIGHLAND SWORDS
THE SCOT'S BETRAYAL
THE SCOT'S SPY
THE SCOT'S PURSUIT
THE SCOT'S QUEST
THE SCOT'S DECEPTION
THE SCOT'S ANGEL

HIGHLAND HEALERS
THE CURSE OF BLACK ISLE
THE WITCH OF BLACK ISLE
THE SCOURGE OF BLACK ISLE
THE GHOSTS OF BLACK ISLE
THE GIFT OF BLACK ISLE

#4-JOURNEY TO THE HIGHLANDS-
Robbie and Caralyn
#5-HIGHLAND SPARKS-Logan and
Gwyneth
#6-MY DESPERATE HIGHLANDER-
Micheil and Diana
#7-THE BRIGHTEST STAR IN THE
HIGHLANDS-Jennie and Aedan
#8- HIGHLAND HARMONY-Avelina and
Drew
#9-YULETIDE ANGELS

THE SOULMATE CHRONICLES TRILOGY
#1 TRUSTING A HIGHLANDER
#2 TRUSTING A SCOT
#3 TRUSTING A CHIEFTAIN

STAND-ALONE BOOKS
ESCAPE TO THE HIGHLANDS
THE BANISHED HIGHLANDER
REFORMING THE DUKE-REGENCY
WOLF AND THE WILD SCOTS
FALLING FOR THE CHIEFTAIN-3RD in a
collaborative trilogy
HIGHLAND SECRETS –3rd in a collaborative
trilogy

THE SUMMERHILL SERIES-
CONTEMPORARY ROMANCE
#1-ONE SUMMERHILL DAY
#2-A FRESH START FOR TWO
#3-THREE REASONS TO LOVE

ABOUT THE AUTHOR

KEIRA MONTCLAIR IS the pen name of an author who lives in South Carolina with her husband. She loves to write fast-paced, emotional romance, especially with children as secondary characters.

When she's not writing, she loves to spend time with her grandchildren. She's worked as a high school math teacher, a registered nurse, and an office manager. She loves ballet, mathematics, puzzles, learning anything new, and creating new characters for her readers to fall in love with.

She writes historical romantic suspense. Her best-selling series is a family saga that follows two medieval Scottish clans through four generations and now numbers over thirty books.

Contact her through her website:
keiramontclair.com.

Made in the USA
Las Vegas, NV
30 December 2024

15627907R00164